The God
of Discord

and Other Weird Tales

Steven E. Wedel

MoonHowler
Press

ISBN: 0692466770
ISBN-13: 978-0692466773

DEDICATION

When I was a teenager in the 1980s my bedroom was decorated with various blacklight posters of the Grim Reaper, along with depictions of Iron Maiden's mascot Eddie and various other monsters. My dad once came into my room, looked around, and said it looked like something right out of Hell. I wanted to thank him, but he didn't mean it as a compliment. I'm sure he thought – and probably still thinks -- my interest in dark things isn't healthy. But can we appreciate the light before we've stood in the darkness? Anyway, this one is for you, Dad.

CONTENTS

The God of Discord

My daughter was bad luck from the very beginning. She was conceived in the backseat of a 1976 Monte Carlo when I was seventeen years old. At the time, I was sure she had ruined my chances of ever amounting to something. Still, I didn't think she could bring about the end of the human race.

But that's possible now that ... now that we've been noticed.

It wasn't Tina's fault. Not that it matters anymore. She's dead. We killed her a couple of days ago. She's stinking up the apartment now. Her heart is drying up and shriveling on a Corningware plate on her bedside table. The cockroaches have enjoyed the feast. I keep her body covered. I can't stand the thought of the roaches getting into her ruined body.

The smell of her burned lungs is still pretty strong in here. When the neighbors came knocking, I told them Lori, my wife, had burned our dinner.

Tina was a mistake and a pain in the ass most of the time, but I loved her. She never meant to do wrong. She was just stupid. She was like her mother that way.

My wife is hanging by her neck over our bed. I disemboweled her, letting her guts slide in a slippery, glistening pile onto our bed sheet.

1

Still, it isn't enough. *He* has seen it all. *He* has watched my sacrifices. *He* approves, but he will not be satisfied. He is coming. He is eternal, older than language. And he's tone deaf.

I am sitting here, watching him watching me as he moves through the universe toward Earth, toward Man, toward me and the end of all that I have ever known. I will record my tale and then I will die – an appetizer for a god. It's better than dying in an industrial accident or being run over in the street.

Tina is – was – in seventh grade. She was in the Longfellow Junior High School marching band. She plays – played – the clarinet. She wasn't good at it. She was terrible. I used to thank the God I once believed in that I got her clarinet for just $25 in a pawnshop and didn't pay hundreds for an instrument I knew she'd never master. She began playing last year, in the sixth grade, at Coolidge Elementary School. I don't know why she ever got into the band. She always hated sucking on that clarinet's wooden reed. I guess she didn't know about the reed when she chose the instrument.

I only have two Valium pills left. The damn doctor won't prescribe any more until the end of the month. The other pills, the red ones I use to supplement my Valium supply, are all gone. Rudy won't sell me any more because I owe him money. I wish I could take these last pills and go to sleep. But, even when I close my eyes, I see the god's eye in the dark, looking into my soul …

I'm not there yet. I'll come to that soon enough.

Tina was horrible on that clarinet. The first year, she practiced every night for at least an hour. It sounded as if she were slowly squeezing the life out of a kitten with a very high voice. I had to leave the house a lot because I just couldn't stand to hear the cacophony she made. I get migraines so easily, anyway, and hearing her torture that instrument always set me off.

She didn't practice much over the summer, but picked it up again once school started in the fall. I wouldn't have believed her ability could have deteriorated if I hadn't heard the sound for myself. I considered smashing the clarinet to bits and pieces when she left it home one day when there was no band class at school. I couldn't do it, though.

That's right, world. I couldn't do it. It would have broken my little girl's heart. Well, that heart is turning black and hard on a dinner plate now and we may all be doomed because I didn't have the balls to smash a clarinet.

On December 21, the first day of winter, Tina was practicing for a concert the band put on during the last day of school before the big Christmas break. She was playing – trying to play – "Silent Night." She hit a series of wrong notes that made every hair on my body stand on end. A chill passed through me – a chill that seemed to turn my bone marrow to slush. I looked at my wife and saw that she also felt it. Her hair was standing up and I guess the sudden chill made her wet herself. Lori never had good bladder control after the pregnancy.

Oh, but the strangeness was just beginning.

The apartment building seemed to … stretch and groan, like a man waking up after a long nap. The hallway outside our apartment filled with people running toward the stairs and I heard the word "earthquake" several times over the agonized sounds of straining wood and cracking brick.

Tina ran out of her bedroom, the accursed clarinet still in her hand. Her hair – her stringy reddish-blonde hair – was white. Her skin was like a marble statue, as if all the pigments had been sucked right out of her flesh. The spattering of freckles on her nose stood out like drops of old motor oil. She tried to say something, but when she opened her mouth it was full of blood.

"Oh my dear God!" Lori shouted. She ran to Tina and got there before I could. She made Tina open her mouth, asking her all the time if the reed had cut her, had she bit her tongue, did something fall on her, had Daddy hit her again ... what happened?

Tina's teeth fell out when she opened her mouth that time. There was more blood. A lot of blood. Or maybe it just looked that way because it was mixed with so much saliva. It seemed like a lot at the time. The stains are still on the carpet.

We ran out into the hall with Tina. We had to get her to a doctor. The building was still groaning and trembling. The hallway was empty, but we found most of the people from our floor and the six floors above us crammed into the stairwell. It took us forty-five minutes to go down five flights of stairs, then another two hours to get through the panicked streets to the hospital, which is just eight miles from here. By that time, Tina's mouth had stopped bleeding and she'd fallen asleep in Lori's arms in the back seat of the car.

The doctor couldn't tell us anything. He was just a kid – still had pimples on his face and probably couldn't have grown more than peach fuzz on his chin if he tried for a week. He said he'd never heard of such a thing but guessed it was probably related to her diet. Tina was skinny, but she ate like a horse and didn't gripe if you gave her vegetables or candy bars; it was all the same to her.

The world changed that night. Do you remember it? Those assholes in Washington, D.C. have been trying to cover it up, but I saw the stars falling, felt the earthquakes and smelled the rising oceans and the stink of the famine dead. I know the world changed that night.

No one – not even me – knew that my daughter had attracted the attention of an entity that had never before taken notice of this spinning little ball in the universe. No one knew that we were now being watched. No one knew that he would come for us.

But he is. I first saw him the night after Tina made her musical mistake. I was sitting on the narrow ledge our landlord calls a patio. Tina was in her room, crying over her missing teeth and the fact she couldn't play in the band concert because the lack of teeth made it impossible for her to blow in that damnable instrument. I got tired of her wailing and, instead of whipping her for making all the noise; I put on my coat and went out to the patio.

I was sitting in a chair out there, not doing anything, really. I took a long drink of Bacardi – I'm a working man, or, at least I was before the damn layoffs – and I deserve to have a moderate drink if I want one. I took a drink, tipping my head back … and saw the red eye looking down at me.

I spewed rum over the ledge of the patio and almost dropped the bottle. I couldn't believe what I saw. I looked again, and there it was … a giant, round red eye with a slitted black pupil, like a cat's. It was just out there – in the deep darkness of space. But it was looking at us. Looking at me.

I made Lori come out on the patio and look at it. At first she said she couldn't see it. I finally had to take her head in my hands and point her face toward the eye. I was scared. Maybe I was a little too rough. I didn't mean to bruise her. But, it worked. Once I pointed her in the right direction, she saw that great big fucking eye looking back down at us.

I suggested we call NASA. Lori didn't like that idea. She said people who reported things flying in the sky disappeared if they told the government. She was right, of course. We decided not to do anything. We'd wait and see if the thing was there the next night.

You guessed it. It was there. But it was bigger. No ... not bigger. It was *closer*. The eye was moving toward us. It was more than double the size it had been the night before. Its gaze was so intense I thought I could feel it reaching into me and feeling around, like a laser beam.

This time, I did call NASA. It took me a while to find the toll-free phone number, but I got through. I told them what I saw. A man – a lieutenant, I think – said they'd get some telescopes pointed in the direction I described and see what they could find.

That night, the god got into my mind, into my dreams. His name is Dhargolmet. He told me that. He told me he had heard of my race but he'd always believed we were beneath his notice ... until one of us had played the sweet music that had caught his attention. He said he was coming and he would enslave us and make my race fill the universe with the music he had heard coming from my home.

That music! It was a series of wrong notes bleating through a horn held by an inexperienced child. It was an accident!

But what could I do?

I tuned into the news the next day. I watched CNN for hours, but there was no mention of NASA finding anything unusual. Maybe, I thought, just maybe it had all been an illusion.

Lori took Tina to Wal-Mart to buy some hair dye that day. Lori had convinced herself that Tina's hair turned white because of a peroxide accident ... never mind the earthquakes and other shit I told her had happened.

They also went to the dentist. The dentist took a mold of Tina's mouth to make her a set of false teeth. Tina was happy about it. The dentist promised to have the teeth for her before the break from school was over.

A lot of good they'll do her now.

The eye was not, of course, any illusion. That night it was there again, closer than before. The first night, it had appeared as a thing about the size of my fist. This time it was as big as a tractor tire. It was out there, staring at us, at me, its slitted pupil unblinking, unflinching ... emotionless.

I called NASA again. This time I talked to a woman who was not so sympathetic. She asked if I was under the influence of alcohol or drugs. I slammed the phone down on the bitch.

Lori would hardly even glance out the patio doors. She took a quick look and agreed with me that there was an eye in the sky. The bruises on her face had turned a dark purple and I felt bad about it.

That night, he came to me again in my dream. I begged for mercy. I begged him to spare all of human kind. I begged ...

He told me that as long as one among us existed who could create the music he had heard, he would come for us. He would fill the universe with that sound. The only alternative was a sacrifice made in his name.

Sacrifice ...

We murdered my little girl on Christmas Eve. Lori was reluctant. Sure, she said, she'd seen the red eye watching us, but she hadn't had any visitor in her dreams. No one had told her to kill Tina. She said I might be sick, that maybe I'd been taking too many pills with my rum. She started to get hysterical and I had to ... make her be quiet. I regretted hurting her, especially since her face was still bruised, but what had to be done was bad enough without her screaming that I was crazy.

I ground up two of my Valiums and put them in a glass of Coke for Tina. She was asleep before the glass was half-empty. I carried her to her bed and lay her down as gently as I'd ever done when she was an infant.

Thirty minutes later, I had her heart in my hands. The sweet child never stirred when I came to her with our best butcher knife and a smaller paring knife I got for free after listening to a cutlery demonstration at the local grocery store.

I never knew surgery was so hard. I didn't know how to get through the rib cage. I had to go in through her abdomen. I cut a slit in her soft little tummy and reached into the hot wet wound, working my way up until I found a hard lump that I knew had to be the heart. I pulled. I had to pull hard to bring it low enough to cut it free with the paring knife.

It was so small. So warm and slippery ... that little engine that had kept my girl alive.

I put it on the plate very carefully, then held the plate over my head and said, "Dhargolmet, I offer you this sacrifice. Show mercy on my race." Then I put the plate on Tina's bedside table.

I was about to leave the room to wash my hands when I saw Tina's clarinet case on her dresser. The god had not given any specific instructions on the sacrifice. I realized it wasn't the heart that would please him. It was my little girl's lungs that had produced the air that created that accursed music.

I reached into her belly again, feeling around until I found her lungs. I cut them out. I knew they had to be destroyed, so I took them to the kitchen, put them in a cake pan, poured a bottle of rum into the pan and dropped a match on it.

The heat from that fire was incredible. It was so hot that I felt sure I had taken care of the problem. Mankind was safe! I washed my hands, told the neighbors to fuck off, and went to the patio for a drink.

The slitted red eye was as big as a school bus, like a bright round patch sewn onto the fabric of the night sky. I remember crying. I drank the rest of Tina's Coke and went to bed.

The god laughed at me that night. He said I had destroyed one source of his beautiful music, but my wife could easily produce another. His first task, he said, would be to impregnate her with his own seed so that she would bear a child better able to play the music he loved.

Of course, I couldn't allow that. Lori wouldn't take my Valium-and-Coke cocktail. I had to crack her over the head with a lamp. Groping around in Tina's body had been bad enough, and I had known what I wanted then. I couldn't bring myself to do that to Lori. And, I don't know enough about female biology to know exactly which parts make a baby.

So I put a hook in the ceiling over our bed, tied a rope to it and fastened a noose around her neck. Then I cut her open, like I'd seen a hog cut open in some movie, and everything just sort of slid out and plopped in a sticky, steaming mess on the bed.

I dug around in the stuff until I found some things I didn't recognize. I figured those had to be her reproductive organs, so I burned them in the same pan – now blackened and warped – where I'd burned Tina's lungs.

The neighbors came pounding again. I ignored them. It had been a harrowing few days, so I took a nap.

Dhargolmet came and laughed at me while I was asleep. He was not just a voice and an eye in the darkness of my dream this time. I could see him. He was huge. Bigger than huge. His slimy bulk was a solar system of ropy tentacles that looked like the entrails of my wife and daughter. The tentacles slithered, coiled and unfurled around a body that seemed to be a solid, living piece of nighttime, with that one monstrous burning red eye planted in the center of it, making the darkness all the more black.

I awoke in the early evening. My head ached terribly. I took a Valium, noticing how few of the little blue pills were left. It was still Christmas Day, so I plugged in the lights on our tree, but the little blinking bulbs reminded me of eyes in the dim room, and they made my head hurt more, so I turned them off. Well, I knocked the tree over, which pulled the electric plug out of the wall. The lights were off.

I dreaded the night, but soon it was upon me. As the

light of the sun faded, the red eye of the god became increasingly visible. It was the size of a football field and I was sure I could see it actually growing as it moved closer to Earth. Closer to me.

Praying did no good. I prayed to the God I grew up with, but that didn't help. I prayed to Dhargolmet himself for mercy, but he only laughed into the confusion of my mind. I looked up again and saw that his eye was even closer. The very stars were as insignificant as floating motes of dust that he ignored in his progress toward this planet.

I guess I passed out then. The next thing I remember, I woke up this afternoon, still on the patio, with the afternoon sun shining down on me. I was very cold because I'd gone outside in just my clothes and a jacket. When I began writing this, my hands were almost too stiff to hold the pencil. But, the warmth of the apartment and a fresh bottle of Bacardi have thawed me out.

Not that it matters now. I know what I have to do. I have destroyed the innocent child who played the accidental notes that attracted this monster. I have destroyed the womb from whence she came. The only thing left to do is destroy the man who produced the seed that fertilized that womb and created the girl who played the notes.

Deep night has come. Dhargolmet is close. His great round orb fills my view of the sky. If I do not destroy myself, he will use me to recreate more misguided musicians like my sweet daughter. If I am dead, perhaps he will be without hope and will turn away from the Earth.

Perhaps.

He is watching me now. I feel that he knows what I am

about to do. I can feel that he is nervous and angry. He is shouting into my mind that I should not, that he forbids it. That is all the proof I need that what I am doing is the right thing.

Someday there will be statues to honor me. I will take my place among the saints and martyrs for my willingness to make this final sacrifice to save my fellow man. As it turns out, the mistake made by a daughter who was herself a mistake will turn me into a hero.

I will go to the edge of the balcony now and throw myself into the night sky, toward the watching red eye.

On behalf of my entire family, I apologize for this brush with extinction.

When the Lady of Byblos Calls

Randy Collins awoke needing to piss and wanting to be at the beach. The first was easy enough to remedy; he rolled out of bed and staggered into the bathroom of his home, raised the ring on the toilet and took aim. Spray came off the stream of urine on one side as if pulled away by a magnet, speckling the white toilet with spots of yellow.

"Dammit." Randy shook the last drops out and tucked himself back into his briefs. He grabbed some paper and wiped down the side of the toilet, then sniffed the air and swore he could smell sand and seagulls. He remembered his dream.

It was a vivid dream for a Nebraska corn farmer who'd never been within five hundred miles of an ocean. He had been standing on wet sand in the boxer shorts and T-shirt he wore to bed. Mist swirled around him in the darkness. The sea breathed toward him in whispering waves, promising, promising, promising until finally reaching him and firmly caressing his toes, his ankles and then his knees, urging him forward. And it had felt good, welcoming. Then he woke up needing to piss.

Randy went downstairs and hit the button on the coffeemaker. By the time he was cracking eggs over a warming skillet, the rich smell of coffee had filled the kitchen and he could hear somebody else moving around upstairs. He peeled apart strips of bacon and laid them out to hiss and pop in another frying pan.

"Hi Daddy."

Randy turned around to find April, his eight-year-old daughter, standing in the kitchen doorway. She was wearing her long pajamas with Winnie the Pooh on them, her feet were bare, her long blonde hair disheveled and one fist was rubbing an eye.

"Good morning, sunshine," Randy said. "Want some breakfast?"

"Chocolate doughnuts?"

"Nope. Eggs and bacon, with toast."

"Where's Mommy?"

"Still sleeping, I guess."

April turned and ran away, but was stopped at the stairs where she met her mother. "Mommy, Daddy's trying to cook again," the girl squealed.

Randy smiled as he heard his wife, Michelle, laugh. "Well, let's go see if we can save our food," Michelle said. A moment later, mother and daughter entered the kitchen holding hands.

"You told on me," Randy said, cocking an eyebrow at April.

"I don't like my eggs all black and hard," the girl said.

"And I want bacon that doesn't hurt my teeth," Michelle added. She was wearing her long flannel nightgown and Randy wondered if she'd bothered putting her underwear back on after he'd pushed the gown up to her waist in order to make love to her last night.

"Well then, fine," Randy said. "I'll just leave this woman's work to the women. But I'll have you notice that the coffee smells like it's going mighty fine."

"Uh-huh," Michelle agreed. "But that's because I put the packet and water in the machine last night."

"I'll be in my dressing room," Randy sniffed, then tilted his chin toward the ceiling and strode out of the kitchen, April's laughter trailing behind him.

When Randy came back, dressed in a flannel shirt and overalls, the breakfast was on the table and his female companions were just sitting down to eat. He lowered himself into a chair and sipped his mug of coffee.

"Mommy's eggs are yellow," April said. "Like they're supposed to be."

"Mommy's eggs are yellow," Randy mimicked. "Maybe I like mine black and crunchy."

April stuck out her tongue, then giggled.

"We should take a vacation," Michelle said. "I'd like to see the ocean. We've never been to the coast."

Randy lowered his mug and studied his wife. "What made you think of that?"

"I don't know. I just woke up wanting to see the ocean. We should do it."

"We're just a couple of weeks from harvest time," Randy said. "We can't take a vacation now."

"We could go after harvest," April said.

"You too, huh?" Randy asked.

"I want to go on vacation and play in the sand on the beach," the girl said.

"It'd be fun," Michelle added.

"It's going to be cold by the time harvest is over," Randy argued.

"We could go down to the Gulf of Mexico, or to L.A."

"Michelle, that's a little more than just a daytrip, you know."

"Think about it. Okay?"

"Please Daddy?"

"All right. All right. I'll think about it. Jeez, a man just doesn't have a chance in this house anymore."

The family finished breakfast and Michelle gathered the used dishes while April ran back upstairs to dress for school. When she came down, she and Randy went out to his Ford pickup to wait on the bus. They sat in the cab; Randy started the vehicle and turned on the heater. Soon, they no longer could see their breath puffing out in front of them.

"It's cold early this year," Randy commented.

"Will it snow pretty soon?"

"It better not. We have to get that corn out of the field. The harvest crew won't be here until next week at the earliest."

"I like the snow."

"You can have all the snow God wants to give you, but not until after harvest. Okay?"

"Will we go to the beach, Daddy?"

"I don't know, sunshine. Wouldn't Austin get jealous of all those other boys seeing you in your bikini?"

"DAA-ddy!" She slapped at his arm.

"You thought I didn't know about him, didn't you?"

"He's not my boyfriend anymore. He broke up with me and he loves someone else now."

"Broke up with you? What kind of dumb boy would break up with my baby girl? I guess you'll just have to be daddy's girl forever."

"No."

"You mean you already have another boyfriend?"

"I'm not going to tell you," she said. "There's the

bus!" She threw open her door and jumped out, slamming the door behind her before Randy could tease her anymore. She raced to the end of the driveway and scrambled up the steps of the yellow school bus. Neil, the driver of the bus, waved at Randy before closing the door and pulling away.

"Little booger's just growing up too damn fast," Randy said, grinning. He left the pickup running and went back into the house, where Michelle handed him a thermos of coffee and kissed him. Randy ran a hand down her back and squeezed her butt through the flannel gown, noting that the underwear was in place. She still smelled warm and comfortable, as if the luxury of sleep was trapped like a fragrance in her hair.

"Want a quick repeat of last night?" he asked, starting to pull up the gown.

"Get out, you horndog." Michelle pushed him away.

"I should be in the store for lunch," Randy said. "I'll expect something hot and inviting. And you can have some food ready, too."

"Out, you pervert!"

Randy went back to the truck, poured some coffee into the thermos lid that doubled as a silver cup, and dropped the pickup into gear. As he waited for a couple of cars to pass on the narrow state highway that ran by his house, he flicked on the radio of the truck and sipped coffee during commercials. He owned just under one thousand acres of land in central Nebraska, more than half of which had been in his family for three generations. He'd added three hundred forty acres to the spread five years ago when old George Maynard retired and moved to Florida. Most of the land was planted in corn, though he'd left the new acquisition devoted to wheat because old George had done so well with it.

Randy pulled the truck onto the highway and headed toward the farthest end of his kingdom. On his left, his own corn stood tall and straight, the long green leaves unmoving in the morning stillness. The corn on the right side of the highway was a few inches shorter and Randy could see holes in the leaves where bugs had been at it. He smiled despite himself.

"Told Bill he ought to invest in more fertilizer and better pesticide," he said. "And water. Corn's gotta have water in the summer."

A Garth Brooks song faded out on the radio and the morning news came on. Randy turned up the volume.

"Breaking news this morning from southern California, where cult members have committed a mass suicide," the announcer said. "About three dozen people, including twelve women and ten children, chartered a yacht yesterday evening. When the boat didn't return on time, the owner notified the Coast Guard, who found the yacht abandoned about fifty miles off the coast of Los Angeles. A journal found on board, apparently written by cult leader Lenora Godwin, says the group has given themselves back to the lady who gave them life. Coast Guard officials say they believe the cult members jumped overboard during the night. Only about a dozen bodies have been recovered so far."

"Only in California," Randy muttered. "Freaking nuts. Shouldn't be allowed to have kids."

The announcer switched to talk about the upcoming gubernatorial elections and Randy tuned it out; he always voted a straight Republican ticket and didn't need to hear who was throwing what mud at whom. He left the highway and started north on a gravel road that soon became a dirt road. A quarter of a mile later he was parked in front of the gate that opened onto the northernmost section of his land. He hopped out of the truck, unlocked and opened the gate, and was back in the cab in time to catch the weather report.

"It's a chilly one out there this morning," the weather announcer said. "But it'll warm up as the sun climbs. Temperatures this afternoon should top off just a couple degrees below normal, with no chance of rainfall today. A ridge of warmer air will be pushing across the state this evening and into tomorrow, bringing our temperatures back up, but increasing our rain chances as we head into the weekend."

Randy drove through the gate and killed the truck's engine. He finished off his cup of coffee and stepped out to be with his crop. Only about a twenty-yard patch just inside the gate wasn't planted with corn. Randy took his .22 rifle from the gun rack over his back window, grabbed a burlap bag from the bed of the truck, and entered the corn, the gun held loosely at his side.

He zigzagged through the crop, stopping every thirty feet or so to feel the firmness and check the circumference of an ear of corn. He held leaves between his fingers, checking textures, looking for evidence of pests, and moved on. Randy walked until he found himself at a fence. He recognized it as the western boundary of his property, so he walked along the fence line for a while, until he spotted movement.

"I've got you now, you son of a bitch," he whispered, raising the rifle to his shoulder and aiming at the waddling shape of a raccoon moving from stalk to stalk, trying to reach an ear of corn and bending the stalks in his attempts. Randy squeezed the trigger. The varmint jumped, waddled quickly for a few feet, then stopped and never moved again on its own. Randy bagged the body and went to sling it over his shoulder, but the bag slipped. Trying to catch the bag, Randy dragged his hand across one of the two rows of barbed wire strung across the top of his fence.

He picked up the bag and more carefully settled it over his left shoulder, then looked at his hand. There was a small, shallow cut just behind the thumb. A little blood was leaking from the wound, but nothing to be concerned about. Randy was about to let the matter go when he realized the blood was not flowing down the back of his hand. Instead, it was moving horizontally, toward his thumb, which was pointing west.

"Damnedest thing I ever saw," he muttered. He quickly wiped the blood onto the thigh of his overalls, picked up his rifle, adjusted the burlap bag and moved on.

He cut straight through the corn for several dozen yards before zigzagging back toward his waiting truck, again checking his crop as he went. Once there, Randy threw the burlap bag and its contents into the Ford's bed. Back in the truck, he'd left the radio on and it came alive when he turned the key.

"Are all these events related to one another?" a woman's voice asked.

"They could well be," a man answered. "Goddess cults have increased in prevalence since the 1960s, but it's too early to tell if all the events last night are related to one another, or even to cult activity."

"Do you expect more of this behavior?"

"I can't answer that," the man responded. "I simply don't know."

"Kirsten Gregory, reporting live from Baltimore," the woman said.

"What the hell's going on?" Randy wondered aloud.

"There you have it," the usual morning newscaster said. "Five bizarre mass suicides last night. In each case, the victims threw themselves into the ocean and drowned. The death toll right now stands at roughly two hundred as Coast Guard crews work to retrieve bodies from the Atlantic, Pacific and the Gulf coast. Stay tuned and we'll keep you up to date on this truly bizarre event."

Randy snapped the radio off and stared at it for a moment. *Fucking weird.* He backed his truck onto the dirt road and went back to lock the gate. He drove to another section of his land and repeated the check of his crop, this time not finding anything to shoot at, though there was evidence something had been gnawing on the base of several stalks.

At noon, he was in the town of Plymouth, sitting on a barstool, his elbows on the lunch counter of the drug store café, watching Michelle serve food to the people who had arrived ahead of him.

"Have you heard the news?" Michelle whispered when she put Randy's usual cheeseburger and fries with a Dr Pepper on the counter in front of him.

"You mean about those cult people drowning? Yeah, I heard."

"Isn't that the strangest thing?"

"Sure is," he said, biting into the sandwich. Michelle shook her head and moved away to wait on an elderly couple that had just sat down.

After lunch, Randy went home and spent the afternoon tinkering with farm equipment and reading up on the benefits of planting soybeans. Michelle and April arrived home at about the same time and they all went into the house. As Michelle began preparing dinner, Randy turned on the news.

"The death toll continues to rise in what many experts are calling the largest mass suicide in modern history," Dan Rather's current backup newsman said grimly. "Fourteen groups, nearly eight hundred people, drowning themselves in the oceans off the coasts of America. An unbelievable occurrence that is, strangely enough, not isolated to this nation. Nearly every coastal country on the globe has reported a similar incident today. There is no way we can gage the exact number of dead as various agencies work to retrieve bodies from the water."

"Oh my God." Randy turned to find Michelle standing in the kitchen doorway, a grease-coated spatula in one hand, her other hand over her mouth. "What's going on?"

"I don't know, but you can forget about that vacation," Randy said.

"We are getting new reports from Virginia Beach," the newsman said. "As the evening tide comes in, hundreds of people are advancing on the shore and walking into the ocean. Cameron Mercer is live on the scene. Cameron?"

"Thanks Ted." A young man with dark hair came on the screen. His attention was torn between the camera and what was happening behind him. "As you can see over my shoulder here, people are literally just walking into the ocean, going as far as they can, then going under. This is so incredible. I don't know what to say. Local police were on the scene earlier, trying to hold people back, but then, one by one, the police officers also turned and walked into the tide. I don't –"

"Cameron, let me interrupt for just a moment," the older announcer cut in. The screen divided so that viewers could see the young man on the scene and the older man in a studio somewhere. "Did you say the police committed suicide, too?"

"Yes Ted, that's right. It's very... very strange, Ted. It's like... I don't know. The sea. It's like the sea is calling..."

The young man dropped his microphone and turned away from the camera. He began to walk away as Ted called after him. Cameron Mercer was soon lost in a crowd of bodies moving slowly toward the ocean that rolled in from the horizon.

"I cannot believe what I'm seeing here," Ted said. "Don't we have anybody else on the scene to stop him? Who's running that fucking camera? What the f—" Ted was abruptly replaced by a commercial.

"He said a bad word."

Randy and Michelle both were startled by April's comment. They pulled their attention away from the ad for cellular phone service and looked at their daughter.

"Yes, he sure did," Randy said. "I bet he gets in trouble for it, too." He turned off the television, flicking a glance toward Michelle to see if she'd object. She turned away and went back to the kitchen.

They had pork chops and fried potatoes for dinner. Then Randy helped April with her math homework while Michelle did the dishes. When the evening chores were finished, Michelle turned the television on again, hoping to watch the usual primetime shows, but every network station and all the cable news stations were showing coverage of more people walking into the oceans all over the world.

"Why are they doing it?" Michelle asked.

"I have no idea," Randy answered. "Turn it off. We don't want visitors tonight." He rolled his eyes toward April, who also was watching the live news footage. She scared easily, which meant she'd come to her parents' bed for comfort. The queen bed just wasn't big enough for three anymore.

"Let's play a game," Randy said. "Sunshine, why don't you run upstairs and get that Chutes and Ladders game I always beat you at?"

"I beat you," she said, jumping up from her spot on the floor and racing toward the stairs.

"How many people do you think are dead?"

"I don't know, Michelle. Looks like a lot. Thousands."

"I have a headache. It's been building all day."

"I've sort of had one, too," Randy admitted. "Came on while I was reading. Did you take anything?"

"Couple of Tylenol. You?"

"No. Figured it'd pass, but I guess I'll take something before I start sliding down those chutes." He got up from the couch and went to the medicine cabinet in the bathroom, where he shook a couple of aspirin into his palm and swallowed them with a handful of water from the sink. When he got back into the living room, April and Michelle had the board game set up. They played three games, Randy making sure he lost each time, then April took her bath and went to bed.

Randy turned on the television again, but before the picture had come on, Michelle said, "Don't. Please?"

Randy turned the set off.

"My headache's worse," she said. "And, I don't know, but I feel bloated or something."

"Uh-oh, that time of the month already? I thought you just did that a couple of weeks ago."

"I did. I'm going to go shower."

"Need any company?"

"I have a headache."

Randy watched her go up the stairs. When she was locked away in the bathroom, he turned on the television again. He found a panel discussion on CNN and paused to watch it. A balding man with a thick nose was talking. The station identified him as Dr. Phil Rosenthal, author of a book called Body of Water.

"The human body evolved from a species that was given life in the water," the professor was saying vehemently. "The role water plays in the body of every living species, including man, has not changed in hundreds of thousands of years. It is integral to our cell function."

"This is preposterous," another panel member, a woman identified as Tanya Robi, press secretary for the department of homeland security, argued. "Just what are you saying, Doctor?"

"Humanity, like all life, crawled onto land from the sea," the professor said, rubbing one liver-spotted hand from his nose up to his forehead and over his shiny scalp. "Our blood is eighty-three percent water. Our heart is over seventy-nine percent water. Our very brains are seventy-four-point-eight percent water. Even the makeup of our bones is almost one-quarter water. The body of a man is about sixty percent water and your average woman is roughly fifty percent water. A child can be up to seventy-five percent water."

"She's calling us home," the third and final panel member said. "She wants us to come back to her. Back to her bosom. The sea is her breast." The TV text said the dreamy-eyed speaker was Lisa Adams, high priestess of Astarte's Temple, based in Detroit. "The Great Mother wants her children to come home."

"Doctor, how do you respond to that?" the moderator, a middle-aged male news anchor, asked.

"You're not giving her any credibility, are you?" Robi nearly shrieked.

"I don't profess any belief in Astarte," Rosenthal said. "I've been a devout atheist since 1971. But something is drawing us toward the sea. I feel it right now, as I'm sure all of you do, as well. An overwhelming urge to drop everything and go to salt water. Something is calling us back to our essence."

"Ms. Adams, who is Astarte?" the moderator asked.

"She is the goddess. The Enduring Star, sometimes called Astarte, sometimes Ishtar, Irdrani, Hathor and other names. She is the most ancient, most powerful of all the gods and goddesses, the Lady of Byblos, Queen of the Stars. She – "

"If I may interrupt," Rosenthal cut in. "Astarte was a goddess worshipped by many people under different names in the ancient Middle East. She was a moon goddess, patroness of Byblos, a thriving port city. Her name changed as her worshippers were conquered. She was last known as Venus by the Romans. It's all bunk. The composition of our bodies is what's drawing us back to the sea, not some ancient goddess. We are like tiny puddles running toward the source from which we splashed."

"Doctor, is there anything that can be done to stop what's happening?"

"Lock yourselves in somewhere you can't escape. I'm not even sure that would work. Can we do that to ourselves? Do we want to?"

"Are you saying – "

Randy turned off the television as the bathroom door upstairs opened and Michelle stepped out, drying her hair in a towel. Randy called that he was coming up, turned off the downstairs lights and went upstairs to take his own shower as Michelle went on to bed. Randy found himself standing in the tub, watching the water run off his body and down the drain. Where is it going? He shut off the faucet, dried himself and went to bed.

Two hours later he was awakened by April pulling the blankets off his bed. Michelle sat up first. "What is it? What's wrong?" she asked.

"We have to go," April answered.

Randy sat up. His head throbbed. His heart seemed to be beating too fast and his vision swam. "Yes, we have to go," he said.

"What? Where?" Michelle demanded.

"Let's go," Randy said. He took Michelle by an arm and pulled her up from the bed. April had his other hand and dragged her parents toward the bedroom door. Randy slipped into his boots, still wearing his pajamas, and snatched his keys from the dresser as he pushed Michelle gently in front of him. "We'll take the truck."

In the pickup, Randy pulled onto the highway and headed west, driving fast. Now that they were moving, his headache seemed to have subsided a little and he was able to breathe easier; his heart rate wasn't noticeable, so he guessed it had returned to normal.

"We're going to the ocean, aren't we?" Michelle asked.

Randy only looked at her. His mouth worked, but he couldn't answer. He hadn't known where they were going when he ushered them into the cab of the Ford, but now that it was spoken, he knew she was right. They were headed for the Pacific.

Michelle soon fell asleep, her head rested against the closed window of the passenger-side door. Randy pushed a compact disc into the player and Charlie Daniels filled the cab with the sound of fiddle music. April fidgeted in the seat between Randy and his sleeping wife, alternately trying to sleep or peer over the dashboard at the road unraveling in the truck's headlights.

"Daddy, what's this?"

Randy turned down the stereo volume and looked at April's left arm, which she was holding out before her, pointing at something with her right. At first, Randy didn't see anything, so he turned on the cab's dome light and looked again. Two lumps, like cysts, had risen on April's arm, the first about a half-inch above her wrist and the other about an inch higher and just a little more toward the inside of the arm.

"I don't know, sunshine. Do they hurt?"

"No. They just feel all squishy." She pushed on one, making an indentation in the crown. Randy watched as the lump reformed to its original shape as if being re-inflated. He reached over and gently felt the lumps. Like April had said, they felt spongy... hard, but giving, like an overfilled waterbed.

"When we get to where we're going, we'll visit a

doctor," Randy told her. He turned off the dome light.

An hour later, Randy noticed the first lumps on his own arms. There were three of them showing on his wrists where they came out of the cuffs of his flannel shirt. He gently felt them and they were exactly like April's. He glanced over at his daughter. She was sitting straight up, her hands folded in her lap, her eyes wide and staring intently forward.

"We have to hurry, Daddy. Hurry." She never looked at him as she spoke.

Even in the dimness of the pickup's cab, Randy could see the lumps that had risen on her throat and beneath her left ear. "We're hurrying, sunshine," he said.

"I can't sit still, Daddy," April whined. "We're not going fast enough."

"We're going as fast as I can," Randy said, noticing for the first time that he had the Ford up to eighty-five miles an hour. He, too, felt restless, as if the very molecules of his being were surging within him, driving him like he was driving the pickup.

The low-fuel light flickered and began to shine on the pickup's dashboard. Randy drove for a couple more miles until he found an exit with a gas station. He pulled to the bank of pumps and killed the engine. Michelle woke up when the movement of the vehicle stopped. Randy pulled his wallet from his pocket and passed three twenty-dollar bills toward his wife. "You want to go pay while I pump? That should fill us up."

"I'm scared," Michelle whispered. "I was dreaming. I'm scared. We should go back."

Something within him rebelled at the thought of turning back inland. "Go back?" Randy shouted. "We can't go back. We have to go on. Now get your ass in there and pay for the damn gas!"

"Hurry up, Mommy," April begged.

"This is wrong," Michelle said, opening her door and looking back at them as if her family had become a couple of dangerous aliens. "I feel it, too, but I know it's wrong." She turned and hurried toward the store when Randy opened his mouth to shout again.

Randy found he couldn't stand still as he pumped gas into the truck's dual twenty-five-gallon tanks. He rocked where he stood, put his hands in his pockets, pulled them out, paced in tight circles, and finally got back into the truck. He started the engine and dropped the gearshift into drive, pulling away from the gas station, ripping the hose and nozzle from the gas pump and sending a stream of fuel glistening under the lights of the station.

"What about Mommy?" April asked as Randy maneuvered back onto the highway.

"She'll find her own way. Everyone will find their own way," Randy said.

They drove. April fidgeted more and more by the minute, finally unlatching her seatbelt and leaning forward so that her hands were pressed against the windshield, her face inches from the glass as they sped along the highway. Behind them, the sun came over the horizon, throwing soft light into the cab of the truck.

"Daddy, I don't think I can wait," April said.

Randy turned to look at his daughter. He felt strung out, as if he had a horrible hangover. His head throbbed and he felt sluggish. His sensed cleared somewhat at the sight of his little girl's face. She looked like a white raspberry. Her delicate face was a cluster of those cyst-like lumps Randy had seen on both their arms. Her throat and neck were covered with the knobs. He looked to her arms and saw that they, too, were covered in bumps.

"Oh sunshine. We have to – "

"Daaaaaaaddeee!"

She burst before his eyes. One moment she was there, her face contorted in terrible pain as she screamed for him, then, for a brief moment she was a spray of pink fluid before becoming nothing but splotches and stains spread throughout the cab of the pickup.

"April! April! April." Randy said her name over and over, as if the repetition would make the runny globs reform into his daughter. "I'll get you there, sunshine. We'll get there."

The sun rose high over Randy as he raced along the highway, and came down in front of him as the day wore on, bathing the horizon in orange. He stared doggedly forward, taking no note of the pedestrians that were lining the interstate now, their swollen, lumpy thumbs held toward him. His own hands were masses of bulges gripping the truck's steering wheel. He'd watched many of the knobs rise on his flesh; they didn't hurt, though they had begun to itch. As the sun sank and the moon rose, the lumps began to throb and pulse, driving him on.

Halfway across Oregon the interstate became choked with abandoned cars and trucks. Randy veered off the road, ran down a fence and kept heading west. Eventually, the terrain became too rough, the deserted vehicles of those who had lived closer to the shore too numerous to get around, and Randy had to stop. He got out of his Ford and started to walk away, but some tiny piece of his mind that was still his own pulled him back. He reached out with one hand that was so bloated the fingers were almost indeterminate. He scooped up a wad of the goo that had been April and clenched it as tightly as his deformed hand would allow. Then he continued west on foot.

The smell of salt water reached inland and drove him faster. Randy's boots were very tight and hurt his feet. He knew they hurt because they, like his hands, had become much larger due to the swelling. He couldn't stop long enough to take off the boots. He hurried on. Finally, he climbed a small hill and the black ocean stretched out before him as far as his swollen eyes could see. The tide was in, but even Randy, who had lived all his life in Nebraska, could tell something was wrong. He moved forward, and finally realized the sound of the water was muffled because the sea was full of bodies.

The corpses of those who had arrived before him shifted and rolled gently as the tide pushed toward the shore. Randy stepped among them, pushing them aside, moving toward the sea, finally clambering over the dead, crawling forward over a solid mass of bodies, the bit of April he carried sticking to his hand like so much mucus as he fought to get over the corpses and into the ocean. As he got further from the shore, the bodies were fewer and moved away when he pushed at them. He slid back into the water.

"I'm here. I've come," he called out, not knowing to whom he called. Around him, other people did the same, while behind them more people came over the bodies of the dead. "I made it. I'm here! I brought April with me." Randy held up his swollen hand with the pink jelly plastered to the bumpy skin. All the while, his feet kept moving him deeper into the water.

Without warning, the darkness before him seemed to shimmer and become very warm. A figure he could not see but could feel like a blast from a furnace rose up from the depths of the sea. Up and up, pulling Randy's eyes with it until he was looking almost straight above himself. A translucent outline towered above him, gigantic, feminine, crowned with the crescent moon and robed in the starry night sky. Randy suddenly felt safe and comfortable, more so than he could ever remember feeling before. The ocean around him became the fluid of his mother's womb, protecting him, nurturing him, calling him home, home where life began.

He clutched the sticky mess that was his daughter to his chest and sank into the serenity of the sea.

Lulu

Angela McDonald waited until the carnie tucked himself into his dirty jeans before she stood and brushed the dirt and dead grass from her knees. It was getting a little too cool to wear short skirts, but showing some leg helped attract the paying customers. She wiped her hand across her mouth and wished for a swallow of cold beer. She could smell the stink of burned motor oil and greasy concession stands that hovered like a cloud around the carnival. She figured she probably smelled like him now.

"Forty bucks," she said.

"Forty? You told me thirty." His eyes narrowed, the sweaty flesh creasing and shifting the coat of grime on his face.

"I said thirty if your crotch didn't stink. Trust me buddy, you need a bath."

"Fuck you."

"That'd cost you another fifty."

His unshaven cheeks spread wide in a snaggle-toothed grin. "You gonna be around tomorrow night?"

"I could be," Angela said. "You in town for the rest of the week?"

"Yeah." He pulled a big leather wallet from his back pocket. It was attached to his belt loop by a chain. Angela watched as he rifled through the cash and finally pulled out two limp twenties.

"You've got a lot of money in there, for a carnie," she said.

"We get paid good to work on this carnival. Lobourat takes care of us."

"Really? Maybe I ought to go offer my services to this Mr. Lobourat."

The carnie laughed. "I don't think you'd get anywhere with him. He don't – he don't seem to need no sex." He paused and rubbed his whiskery chin. "You could ask him for a job though. It'd be nice to have you around."

Angela thought about it. Over the man's shoulder and beyond the trailer they stood near she could see the Ferris wheel turning, its many colored lights brightening the sky. She heard screams and squeals as people rode the faster rides. Hucksters called from game booths. Somewhere to the right she heard the steady thrum of a diesel engine sending power to the rides. She looked that way and saw another carnival worker. He opened his fly and sent an arc of piss cascading onto the soil.

"Where does this carnival go?" she asked.

"All over the South, and from North Carolina to Texas and as far north as Nebraska here in the plains states. We go to Florida for the winter. We're heading back that way now that fall's come."

"What kind of job could I get?"

He shrugged. "I don't know. I just run the Scrambler and the Octopus. I don't do no hiring. Some mechanical work, too, but that's about it."

"Where would I find this Mr. Lobourat?"

"He'd be in that trailer by where you come through the gates," the carnie said. "You really gonna ask for a job?"

"I got nothing keeping me here in fucking Windy

Acres, Oklahoma," Angela said. "Why not?"

"You talk to Lobourat, you tell him Leonard sent you." The carnie grinned again. "That's me. Hey, if I put in a good word for you and you get a job, will you give me a free one?"

"I'll think about it." Angela smiled. "But you'll have to wash that dirty dipstick before you ever bring it near me again."

Leonard laughed. "Yeah. All right."

"See ya." Angela stepped beyond the edge of the trailer and faced the glare and sprawl of the carnival. She brushed the last bit of dirt from her knees as she joined the shifting mass of humanity prowling the midway.

Teenagers traveled in packs, many of the girls carrying large stuffed animals, the boys pointing and laughing at various things. Couples pushed baby strollers, stopping to lift the wheels over the dozens of thick black cables that stretched across the ground like hardened blood vessels that had erupted from the earth. Above the glare of the carnival lights, night had deepened. Moths threw themselves against the bare bulbs that kept darkness off the grounds.

Angela ignored the stares her tube top and mini skirt earned her. Game operators called to her, asking her to come score at their booth. She knew the double meaning that was implied. That's how she'd been earning her extra money since the carnival came into town. A girl can pay the rent on a dumpy duplex working at the local fast food joints, but there was nothing like a bunch of horny carnies to provide some easy, extra cash.

The crowd thinned considerably as Angela approached the gates and spotted the trailer Leonard told her about. It was a long black semi-truck trailer that had painted on its sides depictions of various rides and attractions, including an enormously fat woman and a tiny pony. Angela walked around the trailer and found a set of metal steps leading to a door. She went up the steps and knocked.

She had second thoughts for a moment. In fact, she turned away, but then the door opened and a huge, burly bald man in a red T-shirt and tight jeans filled the opening. His eyebrows were gone, replaced with glinting silver studs. He had rings in both nostrils and two in his upper lip. His muscular arms were covered in so many tattoos Angela couldn't begin to determine what any of them were.

"Whaddaya want?" he asked.

"I – I ... Leonard told me I should come see Mr. Lobourat about a job," Angela said. "Is that you?"

"Nope. Come on in." He stepped aside and Angela saw that the interior was dimly lit. The inside walls were bare plywood decorated with various carnival posters. To her right, Angela saw a bed, dresser, refrigerator and microwave. A voice called from her left.

"Who is it, Jacob?"

"A woman," the muscular man answered. "She wants a job."

Angela looked toward the voice. A small lamp spilled light onto a desk covered in papers. Angela could just make out the shadowy form of a person on the other side of the lamp.

"Bring her over here," the man said.

"Go on." Jacob motioned toward the glow, and Angela started walking. Jacob followed at her heels.

"You want a job?" the man behind the desk asked. He

was wearing a white shirt and a black suit coat. His pale face looked all the more angular because of the harsh shadows cast by the desk lamp. White-gloved hands toyed with a pencil on the desk.

"Yes. I think so," Angela said.

"Sit down." The man motioned to a chair beside her. "What's your name?"

She told him.

"How old are you?"

"I'm twenty-two."

"Do you have any ID to prove that?"

Angela reached into the waistband of her skirt and pulled out her driver's license. She held it out and Lobourat took it, studied it, glancing from the photo to her face and back several times. He extended his arm and Angela took it back.

"You have family?"

"No. I never knew my dad. My mom left town a couple of years ago. I don't know where she went."

"No brothers, sisters, cousins, ex-husbands?"

"No. None."

The shadowed face nodded. "I'll pay you two hundred fifty a week, plus room and board, during our season. During the off season, while we're camped in Florida, you'll get one hundred a week with room and board and you can work another job to make extra money."

"Okay. What would I be doing?"

"I need somebody to take care of Lulu."

"Who's that?"

"Our fat lady. She can't do much for herself because of her obesity."

"What would I have to do?"

38

"Mostly make sure she has food. There are other tasks, though, as needed."

"Nothing sexual. I don't do women. Especially fat women."

Lobourat chuckled. "No, nothing sexual. I don't think you're Lulu's type. You accept the job?"

"Yeah, I guess so."

"Jacob will show you to Lulu's trailer. You can begin working immediately. Here." He held a card toward her. "That will allow you to get whatever food you need for yourself and Lulu from my concession stands."

"Thank you."

"We're glad to have you with us." He turned his dark eyes back toward the papers on his desk.

"Come on." Jacob indicated it was time to go, so Angela followed him out. Outside, the sounds seemed even louder after having been in the quiet of the trailer. The lights were brighter and the smells sharper.

"Is it hard work taking care of the fat lady?" Angela asked.

"How the fuck would I know?" Jacob cast a glare over his shoulder as he started away. "You'll be finding out."

Angela followed without saying anymore. This time, as she walked down the midway, there were fewer stares directed at her, most of them staying on the huge, decorated man in front of her. The carnies didn't call to her, but a few did wave as if knowing she was now one of their own. Angela smiled a few times but didn't wave back.

Jacob stopped in front of another trailer similar to the one they'd just left. On the side was a painting of an enormously fat woman in a yellow bikini lounging on her side and waving with one giant hand. "Lulu, the fattest woman on Earth" was painted beside her dark-haired, smiling head.

A line of people stood on the metal steps leading into one end of the trailer. A thin Hispanic man in a University of Miami cap took dollar bills from those filing into the trailer. At the other end, people trickled out in pairs or small groups. Some laughed, some looked disgusted.

"Come on. You can relieve Juan. He's got other things to do." Jacob led Angela up the stairs. People moved out of his way and averted their eyes. At the top of the steps, he addressed the Hispanic man.

"You can go back to the ring toss," Jacob said. "Lulu has a new assistant. She'll take over here."

Juan looked past Jacob and met Angela's eyes. He nodded. She smiled back at him.

"Give her the apron," Jacob said.

Juan untied a blue apron he wore around his waist and handed it to Angela. She tied it around her own waist, conscious that the pockets were full of bills and coins. Juan handed her another stack of bills he'd been holding in his hand, then squeezed past her and went down the steps and into the crowd.

"It's a dollar a head to get in," Jacob said. "No discount for kids or old people. You let any friends in free and you're outta here. Got it?"

"Yeah."

"Carnival closes at midnight. Somebody'll come back and tell you what to do then."

"Okay."

Jacob scowled at her again, the various studs and rings in his face glinting in the colored lights, then he turned and went back down the stairs. Angela watched until his bald head vanished.

"Can we get in now?" a teenage boy asked. He had his arm around a gum-chewing girl.

"Two bucks for the two of you," Angela said. The kid handed her a five and she counted off change.

Time crawled by much slower than the stream of people who wanted to see Lulu. Angela was amazed that there was hardly a moment without a line backed up outside the door of the trailer. She had no idea why so many people would want to see a grossly overweight woman.

"Is she really that fat?" An elderly woman with a cane motioned to the image on the side of the trailer.

"At least," Angela answered, figuring it wouldn't be a good idea to admit she hadn't yet seen Lulu with her own eyes.

"How much does she eat?"

"I couldn't tell you," Angela answered. "But I wouldn't get within arm's length of her."

"Oh, you're joking with me." The old woman's eyes gleamed and she playfully slapped at Angela with a wrinkled, powdery hand.

"Sure." Angela nodded. "That'll be a dollar."

"Anybody ever have sex with her?" A teenage boy wanted to know. He was with three friends. They all laughed that he had the balls to ask such a question.

"Oh yeah, she picks guys out of the crowd," Angela said. "She might take a liking to you. Your friends can hold the rolls of fat off the floor while she rides you."

The boy's grin vanished and his mouth hung open. His friends whooped. Angela collected their money, and they went inside.

At about 11:30, the crowds began to thin. Angela glanced around Lulu's trailer, didn't see anybody who appeared to be approaching, and hurried down the steps and across the midway to the closest concession stand. She showed the worker the card Lobourat had given her and ordered a hot dog and a Coke. She took the food and scurried back to her post.

Eating the hotdog reminded her of Leonard. She bit into the hotdog and washed down the aftertaste of mustard and relish with a swig of soda. She stuffed the last of her meal into her mouth as two young women and a man came up, paid their money, and went into the trailer. The trio turned out to be her last customers.

Ten minutes before midnight, the Hispanic man, Juan, returned. He climbed the steps, his face shiny with sweat.

"How'd you do?" he asked.

"Pretty good, I think," Angela answered. "I haven't counted it. Do I need to do that or does somebody just collect it?"

"I'll take it to Mr. Lobourat for you tonight," Juan said. "Jacob says you have to care for Lulu now." He paused. "You've been inside?"

"No."

Juan nodded. "I'll introduce you."

Angela followed the young man through the door she'd stood guard at for the past several hours. The place was not well lit. The inside was painted white, and there were no posters, pictures or other adornments on the walls. The smell of human sweat and popcorn hung in the air.

"I'm hungry," a female voice called.

Slowly, Angela turned toward the voice. She felt a

hand rise involuntarily to cover her mouth. Her knees felt weak and she wished she could sit down, but there was no chair. She leaned her back against the wall of the trailer. Her eyes were large and round as she stared at Lulu, the fattest woman on Earth.

The woman was an incredible blob of humanity sprawled on the floor of the trailer. The painting on the outside showed a huge woman with a happy face ... a woman who appeared comic in her excessive size. The thing on the floor of the trailer was not funny at all. At first glance Lulu resembled a mound of spilled vanilla pudding. Her flesh was pale and doughy, rippling and sagging as she moved slightly. Her arms and legs stuck out from her torso like plump sausages that had been poked into the mound of pudding. Like in the painting outside the trailer, Lulu wore a yellow bikini. The triangular bits of cloth that made up the bikini top seemed to be keeping two fleshy mudslides from oozing off the top of the pile and onto the floor. The bikini bottom was mostly hidden in rolls and wrinkles of flesh.

Lulu was propped into a sitting position, her back leaning against a wooden ramp that rose at a forty-five degree angle from the trailer floor. There was a table to her right, between her and the wall of the trailer. The table held various food wrappers and a crushed paper cup. On her left was a yellow nylon rope stretching from one end of the trailer to the other to mark where the gawkers who filed past could not go. Angela wondered who in their right mind would ever want to get between the rope and the fat woman.

"I'm hungry," Lulu repeated. Her voice was high and whiney, tinged with something Angela thought sounded like panic.

"I forgot to tell you. She needs more food every couple of hours. It's past her feeding time," Juan said. He then directed his voice to the fat woman.

"Sorry Lulu," he said. "It's my fault. This is Angela. She's your new assistant. She just joined us tonight. She'll take care of you."

"Please feed me," Lulu begged.

Angela forced herself to look Lulu in the face. She found two deep, dark, scared eyes looking back at her. Despite the bulk of the body, Lulu's face seemed very thin and drawn. Her black hair was limp with perspiration and hung around her eyes. The eyes ... Angela couldn't look away from their haunted stare.

"I'll get you something to eat," Angela said.

"Go to Vinny's stand, the green one with the picture of the cotton candy on the sign," Juan said. "Tell him Lulu needs her midnight snack. He'll give you what you need."

Angela left through the entrance door and hurried to the concession stand. The man inside seemed to be all angles and cigarette smoke. He shook his head at her request, then pulled out a plastic bag filled with hot dogs, bits of bun, wads of cotton candy, caramel and candied apples and flecks of buttered popcorn that looked like bits of yellow dandruff. He shoved the bag through the window and waved Angela away.

The bag was heavy and Angela had to carry it with both hands, but she got it back to Lulu's trailer and up the steps. She hesitated, then went inside.

"Oh my God!" She dropped the bag and covered her face.

Juan was kneeling between Lulu's flabby legs. The

bikini bottom was actually only a flap of cloth that must have been tucked into rolls of fat. It was raised and resting on Lulu's belly. Juan was wiping shit off the woman's thighs and genitals with a large white cloth. A plastic pail of steaming, soapy water stood beside him. He dipped his cloth into it and continued to wipe. He glanced over his shoulder at Angela.

"This is your job. I'll do it for you tonight since you're new. In the morning, though, you've got to do it."

"Oh no ... " Angela shook her head. "I can't ... "

"It's not so bad. Like a baby," Juan said. "A very large baby."

Lulu's high, whining voice interrupted. "You brought me some food?"

"Uh-huh," Angela said. Despite her disgust, she could not stop watching Juan as he cleaned between the woman's legs.

"Give me," Lulu said, waving a bloated arm.

Angela picked up the bag and took it to Lulu. She put it on the floor and opened it, then paused before reaching in. Lulu's hand shot forward and delved into the bag. Her arm brushed Angela's, it was soft and cool and dry. Angela stepped out of the way as Lulu brought up a fistful of wieners and cotton candy and stuffed them at her face.

Juan stood and dropped his cloth into the bucket. He pulled down the bikini flap and, just as Angela suspected, simply tucked it into rolls of flesh to cover Lulu's groin.

"She's all yours," he said, then left the trailer, shaking soap suds off his hands as he went.

"Where am I supposed to go," Angela asked. "Where do I sleep?"

"In here. With me," Lulu said, chewing.

"Great." Angela turned away. She felt her own supper rolling in her belly and couldn't bear to watch Lulu eat. She studied runs in the paint of the trailer wall.

"I'm done," Lulu said at last. Her voice had changed.

Angela turned around. The woman seemed calmer. Her eyes still looked very sad, but they no longer appeared so desperate.

"I'm sorry," Angela said. "That was mean of me. I – "

"Everyone does it at first," Lulu said.

"Oh."

"There's a rolled-up mattress and some blankets in that trunk beside the exit," Lulu said. "Those are for you to sleep on. If you want."

"Thanks." Angela went to the exit and found the wooden trunk under the back of Lulu's ramp. She took out the narrow, thin mattress, a flat pillow and ratty blanket. She spread them on the floor and lay down.

"Good night," Lulu called.

"Night."

Angela didn't sleep for a long time. She knew she should get up, walk through the open door, and run as fast as she could. But there was something about Lulu that stopped her from hurting the fat lady's feelings. The thought of those sad brown eyes filling with tears because her assistant had abandoned her held Angela on the mattress. Still, she knew there was no way she could stay. She could never clean the woman's groin the way Juan had done. Angela decided she would sneak out when she was sure Lulu was asleep.

She dozed. Several times she felt her eyelids close and jerk open again. She could not tell if Lulu was asleep.

Surely a woman that fat would snore. But no sound came from the pale mountain of flesh. Angela felt her eyes closing again.

"It's about finished with me."

Angela's head snapped up. "Huh? What?"

"This body," Lulu said. "It's about finished with me."

"What do you mean?"

"I was thin like you when I came to work for Pierre Lobourat. I was Lulu's assistant."

"What? You were ... But ... "

"I know what you're thinking."

Angela rubbed sleep from her eyes. The trailer was darker than it had been when she laid down. The lights were off. It was stuffier, too. She glanced toward the exit and saw that the door had been closed. Slowly, she looked to the other end of the trailer. No light came through the doorway; she guessed the entrance door was also closed.

"Did you close the doors?" Angela asked.

"I think Jacob did that," Lulu answered. Her voice still sounded sad, but now it seemed muffled, too, as if something was blocking her mouth. In the darkness, Angela saw that Lulu was beginning to move. Her massive body pumped forward a few times and then seemed to melt to the side so that she was lying between Angela and the entrance.

The only light coming into the trailer fell through vents along the top of the compartment. It was just enough for Angela to see that Lulu's head was sinking into her shoulders.

"What are you doing? What's happening to you?" Angela asked.

"I told you this body is finished with me," she said.

Her head tilted back as it sank deeper between the shoulders. "My real name is Michelle Winters. I've been stuck here for about six months. Thank God I'm finally going to die. My mother – "

Her head was suddenly sucked into a black hole between the shoulders. The flesh closed over the hole. Angela heard a wet popping sound and smelled excrement as the headless body messed itself.

Then a clammy, doughy hand reached forward and clutched her ankle. Angela screamed and jerked free. She turned to the exit door. It was locked. She began pounding on it and calling for help.

She sensed more than saw Lulu moving toward her. The blob lost its human shape as it neared, becoming more and more just a sliding mass of featureless blubber. It rolled and oozed closer.

Angela screamed and screamed. She sobbed as the thing pooled around her feet and rose up her legs. It was as if her lower body was trapped in quicksand – she couldn't move. She cried and pounded harder on the door. Still the mass rose higher and higher. The pressure against her was heavy and suffocating, like being in deep water. The fleshy substance reached her shoulders, then spread out over her arms so that soon it was not Angela's hands but Lulu's flabby fists pounding on the door of the trailer. Only Angela's head remained above the new coat of oppressive flesh.

Then she felt the stingers penetrating her body. Deep inside the casing of Lulu's body, thousands of tiny darts jabbed into Angela's own flesh. A sudden, deeper jab punctured her abdomen, and something hot and wriggly entered her stomach. Angela screamed with the pain of the invasion.

Then the big thing in her belly began to suck.

Angela felt Lulu's body tense and squirt more shit onto the floor. She didn't care that she was sitting in it. She was suddenly too hungry to care about such mundane matters.

Nocturnal Caress

Last night I visited the Baker house – Pam and Allison Baker of Oklahoma City. I was already under Allison's bed when mother and daughter came home in the evening. I am ancient and I have learned to be patient. I can wait a long, long time before caressing my victims.

I only had to wait a few hours before Allison was mine.

They brought food home with them – hamburgers and fries from a chain restaurant. After eating, Allison came into her bedroom, picked up a ball and a jump rope and went outside to play. Pam stayed in the living room; I could hear the television playing a rerun of *The Simpsons*. Allison was back in the house an hour later. Darkness comes early in the winter.

Sweet, sweet darkness.

Pam went to take a shower. Allison changed the channel on the television and became fascinated by a program about a young woman and her friends who slay vampires. I knew this would happen. It was this premonition that drove me to hide under Allison's bed. Seven-year-old little girls are not meant to watch such shows.

That's exactly what Allison's mother said when she came back from her shower. She changed the television program and sent Allison to get ready for her bath. Allison was sulking when she came in her room to prepare for her bath.

I watched from the safe darkness under her little bed as she took clean pajamas from a dresser drawer. I tingled with pleasure as she removed her shoes and began rummaging in a toy box, searching for something to play with in the bathtub.

Slowly, stealthily, I reached a hand from the safety of the bed. Between her rolled-down pink sock and the cuff of her purple pants a strip of smooth white flesh was visible. Gently, oh so gently, I stroked that little flash of soft skin.

She jumped. They always jump at first. I am ancient and I have learned to be quick. I was back under the bed before the child turned to see what had brushed her ankle. Of course, she didn't see me. She left the room without a toy. She returned to her mother. I heard the conversation.

"Mommy, something grabbed my leg."

"What? When?"

"Just now. In my room. I think it's under my bed."

Yes, they're always sure where I am. They just can't find me. I am ancient and have learned to hide myself well.

"There's nothing under your bed, honey. This is what happens when you watch those scary shows. Now go take your bath."

Allison did as she was told. By the time she returned to her bedroom to brush her long blonde hair, she'd forgotten about me. But I was still there. I was still waiting. Her slight weight settling onto the end of the bed was nothing to me. Her little bare feet dangling three inches above the carpet were everything to me.

Her toes were like little beans. Her feet smooth and still stubby with extreme youth. Her ankles were dimpled and sweet and her calves smooth and round where they vanished into a blue nightgown.

Again, I reached for her. Yes, my touch is cold and dry and I know that it is not a pleasant sensation when I make contact with my human victims. That is of no concern to me. I touched little Allison's right ankle, skimming down the red bottom of her foot to spread her toes.

I should not chuckle at the way she jerked and jumped off the bed. The hairbrush she'd been using fell to the floor and bounced twice on the carpet. Allison, poor dear, was almost crying as she explained to Pam that there really was something under her bed. Really, really.

I saw them coming toward me. Two sets of bare feet, four naked ankles. They paused at the end of the bed. Pam's lovely toenails were painted a soft blue with sprinkles of glitter in the polish. Her hand came down, her long fingers – with nails painted to match her toes – came down and scooped up the dropped hairbrush.

"There's nothing there, Allison," Pam's voice said again.

Then Pam settled to the floor, folding her long bare legs under her – her nightgown was much shorter than that of her chaste little daughter, coming only about halfway down her silky thighs. She raised up the edge of the bedspread and her face looked into mine.

She could not see me, of course. I am ancient and I have learned to become invisible. I studied Pam as she gazed half-heartedly under Allison's bed. She had soft pink lips and large brown eyes. Long blonde hair.

I wanted to touch her, but I knew it was best to wait. I had to finish with Allison first.

"See honey, there's nothing there."

"But something touched me. I felt it," Allison argued.

"There's nothing. Come and look."

"No. I don't want to."

"Come on and get in bed. I'll tuck you in."

I watched Allison's pudgy little feet move around the bed. She didn't let them dangle as she settled onto the bed, but pulled them up quickly. Oh, it was hard not to reach out and touch Pam's lovely ankles with my cold caress. Her very toes came under the shadow of the bed, but still I refrained.

Finally, the mother walked away. She turned off the bedroom light and pulled the door so that it was almost completely closed.

I was alone in the dark with little Allison.

Few children have the ability to lie still when they sleep. Even when they do, it is no matter to me. I am ancient and have learned to control my temperature, which in turn affects the temperature of the air around me. I made myself hot. Very hot. Soon, Allison was tossing around on the bed above me, trying to get out from under the blankets in her sleep.

And then ... her little foot flopped over the side of the bed and hung before me. Tiny blonde hairs were backlit from the sliver of light coming into the bedroom through the space between the door and the jamb.

With trembling fingers, I touched the smallest of her toes, plucked at it like a boy in a berry patch. She twitched but did not pull away. I leaned from the dusty darkness under her bed and softly kissed her ankle. My dry, withered tongue slid between my parched lips and caressed the softness of her instep.

She woke up screaming. I laughed softly and withdrew to the darkness under the bed where I could watch her little feet hit the floor and run from the room.

There was no way, she explained to her mother, that she was going back in there as long as the monster was under her bed. Pam gave up the fight.

"Come on, Allison, you can sleep in my bed with me."

I am ancient and I have learned to move quietly. Allison was already in her mother's bed when I entered Pam's bedroom. Nobody saw me move through the open door. Pam sat on the side of the bed, setting the time on an alarm clock. I scuttled between her soft naked feet to the safety under her bed. She screamed and raised her feet.

"What was that?"

"What happened, Mommy?"

"I thought I felt something run between my feet. Like a cat. Only ... only it didn't feel hairy."

"It's the monster!" Allison yelled.

I laughed until my ancient eyes produced one single tear each.

"There's no monster," Pam said. "Maybe it was just a draft of cold air."

"It's the monster."

"Hush, Allison. Hush. There's no monster. I'll look under the bed."

"No Mommy. He'll get you if you do that."

"Let me go, Allison. I'm going to look."

She did. Pam knelt on the floor and leaned over to look under her own bed, just as she had looked under her daughter's. I was having fun. I reached out with an invisible arm and quickly, lightly traced a finger along the soft line of her jaw.

Oh, she screamed and jumped so high. I laughed and laughed. Allison screamed and I laughed some more.

Pam jumped into the bed and pulled the covers up.

"What happened Mommy? Did you see the monster?"

"Go to sleep," Pam said. "There's nothing under there. I didn't see anything. There's nothing."

Oh no, there's nothing under the bed. Nothing but me. Nothing but Fear. The women remained awake until morning, finally slipping into a light sleep after the sun began lighting the bedroom windows. I slipped away, my work finished, my fun over. Pam and Allison will not forget me for a long time. They may never let their lovely feet linger near the shadows under their beds for fear I will reach out and caress them again.

No matter. There are others. So many other beds, so many other feet.

Tonight I will be in Newport, Oregon. A boy named Daniel McComb is reading a scary story despite his mother's warnings.

I am ancient, and I love disobedient children.

Path of Pins

Webster Gregg once had sex with a chicken. The man who paid him to do it then killed the bird, plucked it, baked it and fed it to his in-laws. Not that Webster knew about that part. By the time the man's mother-in-law bit into the chicken's juicy breast, Webster was passed out in an alley, an empty syringe still clutched in his hand.

Webster was 18 when he seasoned the inside of the chicken. That was 1983. In 2001, he no longer had the boyish good looks he'd had that day. His nose had been broken a few times, a couple of his teeth were missing and his hairline was receding toward the bald spot at the crown of his head. At the age of 36 he was no longer a pretty boy-toy with an addiction, but just an over-the-hill junkie man-whore living on the streets of Oklahoma City.

He woke up cold one morning, huddled beneath the concealing branches of a cedar tree in a park not far from downtown. He opened his eyes and stared across the brown grass. A red squirrel chewed an acorn a few yards from where Webster lay. Webster knew the year was getting late. It would be cold soon.

He rolled from under the cedar branches and got slowly and stiffly to his feet. His veins burned within him, begging for something ... heroin preferably, but some good meth would do the trick. It was all gone, though. All gone. There would be work to do today.

Webster unzipped his fly and hauled his penis out of his Dockers. He'd found the pants in a trash dumpster behind the thrift store on NW 16th Street. They were a couple sizes too big for him, but a piece of cotton rope kept them around his waist. He shot a yellow arc of piss into the cedar tree that had sheltered him all night, tucked himself back into his pants and turned toward the heart of the city.

As he walked, he decided to have breakfast at the Gospel Garden. The morning sermon was always a pain in the ass, but they usually had hot biscuits and gravy. Sometimes they even included a few strips of bacon.

Webster trudged past the first parking lots and low office buildings of the downtown area. He kept the collar of his old thin jacket turned up and didn't look at anybody. A pair of obvious tourists stepped into a doorway to avoid him. Judging from the cameras they carried, he figured they were on their way to the bombing memorial. Getting a handout had been easy the week after the Murrah building got blown up, he remembered. There'd been free food and stuff all over the place.

A car horn blared at him as Webster crossed the street. He didn't look at the driver. He kept walking, past the city's tallest buildings, past the train station, until he came to the little building that was almost under one of the access ramps to Interstate 40. The gravelly voices of a couple of dozen other homeless men seeped through the walls. Webster reached out with an unsteady hand and pulled open the door.

The sound of "Amazing Grace," along with the aroma of sausage and maple syrup, wrapped around him and pulled him into the building. Heated air curled around his legs and wormed its way under his coat. Webster grinned and moved to an empty place at the closest table.

Pastor Troy smiled at him. Webster nodded back, wishing Pastor Don was there instead of Troy. Don was an older man who'd long since given up on converting the homeless people who came to the Gospel Garden for free food and shelter. Pastor Troy was still young and convinced he could make a difference in the world. His before-you-can-eat-you-have-to-listen-to-this sermons were twice as long as Pastor Don's.

Webster's stomach grumbled. His veins still burned. It felt as if they were pushing toward his skin, ready to break free and whip around like rabid snakes in search of the venom that would calm them.

There was some shuffling behind him. Webster looked over his shoulder to see that Lily Dan had moved up to sit beside him. Lily Dan carried a clay flowerpot with him wherever he went. He swore there was an Easter lily planted in the packed soil and that someday it would bloom. His daughter had planted it before she and her mother died in a car accident and Dan's life fell apart. Webster knew there was nothing in the pot but dirt and cigarette butts; he'd dug through the soil one night when Dan was asleep.

"Amazing Grace" ended. The men sat. Pastor Troy began his sermon, waving his new Bible at the men and repeating over and over how Jesus loved them all. Webster rubbed his left wrist where he'd last injected himself. Lily Dan rubbed his flowerpot.

"Somebody's lookin' for ya," Dan said. "I told him about ya, and now he wants to see ya."

"Who?" Webster asked.

"His name is Lou. No ... Luther. That's it."

"What does he want?"

"Favors."

"Oh." Webster thought of that long ago chicken. He still had a reputation as a man who'd do just about anything sexual. "What's he paying?"

"Don't know. Wouldn't tell me 'cause I wouldn't do it," Dan said.

"He said what he wanted done?"

"Yep. I'll tell ya when Pastor Troy runs outta steam. It ain't proper to say while the man's preachin'."

Webster waited. His stomach growled. His veins burned. He fidgeted in his metal folding chair, felt around in his pockets, rubbed his stubbly face and finally sat hunched over his knees, his chin in his hands, wishing for a warm shot of methamphetamine.

Finally, Pastor Troy gave up. Webster glanced around and saw that the other homeless people gathered in the shelter all seemed to have the same glazed-over look he was sure he had. The preacher asked them to bow their heads for a blessing. When the words were done, Webster raised his head and rose from his seat. He filed into line with the other people and was given a plate of food. He sat down and dug into it, Lily Dan beside him again.

"So, what does this guy want? This Luther?" Webster asked.

"He's havin' some kind of party, or sumpin' tonight," Lily Dan said, a fleck of pancake flying from his mouth. He wiped his lips as if apologizing for the projectile. "He wants somebody to ... Well, there's a ... whaddaya call it? Where people have to do sumpin' to join a club?"

"Ritual? Initiation? Hazing?" Webster offered.

"Yeah, yeah. That's it," Lily Dan said, stuffing sausage into his mouth and nodding. "Anyway, he wants you to help with that."

"How?"

"Well, seems these folks gotta kiss somebody," Lily Dan said. Webster noted that his friend refused to look at him. "They gotta kiss somebody right on ... right on the asshole."

"Ah."

"I mean, I ain't one to judge," Dan said. "We all gotta do what we gotta do. It ain't sumpin' I could do, though. I told him that. Then I remembered ... well, you did that thing with the chicken. And other things. I thought maybe you'd do it. He says he'll pay twenty dollars for each person who does it. You know, twenty bucks per kiss?"

"Not bad money," Webster observed.

"I couldn't do it," Lily Dan repeated.

"How do I find this Luther?"

"You mean you're gonna do it?"

"Why not? I could use the money. All I have to do is bend over and let people kiss me. Corporate big shots do it all the time. That's how they get to be big shots – they kiss somebody else's ass until eventually it's them getting kissed on the ass. Maybe this is a promotion for me."

Lily Dan just stared at him, puzzled. Webster laughed. "Don't worry about it, Dan. Just tell me how to find this guy."

"He gave me this." Lily Dan pulled a crisp, bone-white business card from the breast pocket of his battered army jacket. He handed it to Webster.

"Luther Simmons," Webster read. "No title, no business name. Just his name, phone number and a Web site. Interesting. I'll call him. My laptop computer's in the shop, you know."

Dan laughed at the joke, which seemed to break the tension Webster had felt building between them. Lily Dan had no qualms about stealing to sustain himself, but the man was absolutely prudish when it came to performing sex favors for money, food, booze or drugs. Webster finished his breakfast and went to the back office of the Gospel Garden while Lily Dan returned to the chow line.

"Pastor Troy?" Webster asked, stopping in the doorway of the office. The preacher looked up from some papers he was shuffling.

"Yes … Webster, isn't it?"

"Yes sir. Webster. That's me. I was wondering, sir, if I could use the telephone. Dan told me about a man who has a job he needs done. He gave me his number. I wanted to call and find out about doing it."

"Wonderful, Webster. That's great. What kind of work is it?"

"I'm not sure," Webster said. "I think it might be some kind of corporate work. You know, mopping up or something."

"No work is menial, Webster. It all has to be done. Let me gather these things and I'll give you some privacy." Pastor Troy shifted his papers into a stack and left the office.

Webster closed the office door, sat at the desk and picked up the black phone receiver. He punched out the number on the business card.

"This is Luther Simmons," said a deep, sonorous voice.

"Mr. Simmons, my name is Webster Gregg. A friend of mine here at the Gospel Gardens said you need somebody to help you with a party tonight. He said it was … like a kissing booth."

"A kissing booth? What a wonderfully quaint way of putting it," the voice of Luther Simmons said. "I understand your caution in referring to the actual activity, Mr. Gregg. Yes, your friend told you true. Are you interested?"

"It's twenty bucks a kiss, is that right?"

"That is correct."

"And that's all it is? Just a kiss on … down there?"

"Yes, that's all. Unless, of course, you want more. We expect to have quite a party after the initiation. You would be welcome to stay for that, if you wish."

"Will there be food?"

"Oh yes. Food, drinks, sex and more. A real debauchery. I think you'd like it."

"Okay. I'll do it. Where do I meet you?"

"Meet me in front of the Myriad Convention Center in one hour. Some of my guests are particular people, Mr. Webster. I think you might need a bath before the party. And maybe you would enjoy a nap in a real bed?"

"Yes, that would be nice," Webster admitted. "Listen, Mr. Simmons. I … I haven't had anything today. You know, no injections. I – "

"Not to worry, Mr. Gregg. You will be taken care of."

"Thank you. Thanks a lot, Mr. Simmons."

"I will see you in one hour."

The phone went dead in Webster's hand. He hung it up and left the office. Pastor Troy met him at the door.

"Did you get the job?"

"I think so," Webster answered. "I have to meet him in an hour. So I have to go. Thanks for the sermon this morning."

"Go with God, friend," the pastor said.

Webster thanked Lily Dan for providing the information, then slipped out of the Gospel Garden homeless shelter and headed west, toward the convention center. He arrived early, as it was just a twenty-minute walk, and used the time to panhandle some coins from people passing by. He was startled when a long, shiny black limousine glided up to him and a blackened rear window slid down. A pinched face framed with slicked-back black hair and a closely cropped beard and moustache looked up at him. The man's eyes were the darkest Webster had ever seen.

"Webster Gregg, I presume?" the man asked, smiling.

"Maybe," Webster said.

"I am Luther Simmons. Please get in." The face moved out of the frame of the window. Webster opened the door and cautiously got into the backseat, closing the door behind him. The window hummed and closed beside him.

"I didn't expect a limo," Webster said.

"I prefer to travel with a bit of class," Simmons said. "Would you like a drink?"

"Sure." Webster watched as Simmons chose a bottle of amber fluid from a bar built into the back of the car's front seat. Luther Simmons' hands were pale, his fingers long and dainty. He wore a single ring with a black stone on his left pinky. His clothes were all black and didn't seem to have a single wrinkle anywhere. He handed Webster a glass and Webster greedily drank the rich bourbon in a couple of swallows. Simmons refilled the glass.

"I think we will burn your clothes, Mr. Gregg. They do not smell appealing at all," Simmons said. "Have no fear. I will provide you with more suitable garments."

"What kind of party is this you're putting on?" Webster asked, more to change the subject than because he actually cared.

"An old-fashioned Black Sabot," the other man said. "It's Halloween, you know. It's like our Christmas."

"You're devil-worshippers?"

"Is that important to you?"

Webster thought about it. "No, I guess not."

"Good."

They drove on for a while. Webster noticed they were on the Broadway Extension, heading north. Soon they crossed into the Edmond city limits and turned east, passed the college and then turned north near the far edge of town. Finally the car paused at the gates of a housing addition. After a moment, the black iron gates slid apart and the limo passed through. Webster turned and watched the gates close behind them.

"Where are we?" he asked.

"Shadow Run, a housing addition I developed," Simmons answered. "It's a place for my kind of people. Where we don't have to worry about prying neighbors."

"Oh."

"Do not be nervous, Mr. Gregg."

The car stopped again in front of a massive home built of gray stone. Luther Simmons opened his own door and stepped out, offering a hand to help Webster out. The driver remained in the car and drove away when Simmons closed the back door.

"Come inside and let's get you cleaned up," Simmons said.

The inside of the house reminded Webster of pictures he'd seen of museums. There were strange paintings and carvings hanging on the walls, suits of armor and other statues stood guard here and there. The furniture was leather or fur or rich, dark wood and all looked very comfortable and very expensive.

"You like my home?"

"It's nice," Webster answered.

"Here is the bathroom." Simmons opened a door and ushered Webster into a bathroom done completely in black tile and carpet, with the tub, sink and toilet made from black ceramic. Even the faucets gleamed like fresh crude oil. Simmons turned on the taps over the tub and dropped in several cakes that immediately began to fizz and make bubbles in the water. "Take off your clothes and get in. You have soap and shampoo. There are deodorants and colognes in this cabinet." He motioned to an ebony door. "Towels are here." He motioned to another door. "Wash your anus particularly well, Mr. Gregg. I will inspect you thoroughly when you are finished."

The bar of Ivory soap was the only white thing in the bathroom, except the mountains of bubbles that formed in the tub. Webster lowered himself into the warm water, leaned his head back and soaked for a long time. Eventually, he took up the white soap and a black washcloth and began to scrub himself. He leaned back and pushed himself up to scour between his butt cheeks with the washcloth.

As he finished, Luther Simmons returned to the bathroom, entering without knocking.

"Here to check me, I guess?" Webster asked.

"Yes, Mr. Gregg." Simmons smiled.

Webster stood up and turned his back to his host. He bent over and grabbed his ass with both hands. His cheeks were slippery with bubbles, but he spread them apart. He sensed Simmons leaning in close. He heard the man sniff three times.

"Very good," Simmons said. "I will bring you some clothes."

Simmons left and came back a few minutes later with a loose pair of khaki pants, a knit shirt and loafers, all very black. Webster applied deodorant and cologne and dressed in the clothes.

"I have some treats prepared for you in the next room," Simmons said. "Not much. I need you to be lucid this evening. I think you'll find what I have provided now to be sufficient to ease your pain. You will get a much more euphoric feeling tonight."

Simmons took Webster to a bedroom paneled in dark wood. A black table stood before a black wing chair. On the table was a black candle, a tiny spoon, a syringe and a glass vial of white powder. Muted sunlight came into the room through drawn drapes. A king-size bed hunkered against the wall opposite the windows.

"Enjoy yourself. Food will be brought to you later. Sleep, if you wish. Watch television or read a book. Whatever you want," Simmons said. "Likely, I will not see you again before the party tonight."

Simmons left. Webster cooked his junk and sent the hot liquid shooting through his screaming veins. He sighed and leaned back in the black chair. His vision swam and he felt his consciousness spiraling up and away from him.

He awoke sometime later to find that a plate of chilled fruit had been left on the bed. He had a serious case of the munchies, so he fell on the food, devouring orange slices, apple wedges, grapes and cantaloupe with a ravenous appetite.

The food took the edge off his hunger, but having his stomach satisfied only brought the burning in his veins to the forefront of Webster's mind. He rubbed his arm where he'd injected the heroin. He lay back down on the bed, but couldn't sleep; he couldn't stop fidgeting.

Slowly, the room darkened. Webster considered turning on a light, but decided against it. A digital clock beside the bed counted off the minutes with little red lights. Webster rubbed his arm, felt the blood pumping through his veins, and waited.

At 7:30 p.m., the bedroom door opened and a huge, muscled man with a shaved head and thin brown goatee entered the room. The man was dressed in black jeans, black T-shirt and black boots. His head seemed to glow and float above his dark body.

"It's time to go, Mr. Gregg," the man said. "Are you ready?"

"I'm ready," Webster said. He got off the bed and swooned a little when he stood up. He steadied himself and grinned sheepishly at the man. "Looking forward to the refreshments," he said.

The man didn't acknowledge the remark. He simply waved Webster ahead of him and proceeded to give directions. They went downstairs and through the dark house to a back door. The man opened the door and motioned Webster through it.

The light of a huge bonfire blinded Webster for a moment. He rubbed his tear-filled eyes and squinted ahead of him. A group of people sat to one side of the fire, playing drums, flutes and guitars. Other people danced around the fire. Most of the dancers were naked. Webster guessed there to be at least twenty dancers. More people milled around the yard or clustered in small groups.

"Please remove your clothing, Mr. Gregg," the bald guide said.

"Huh? Oh. Yeah." Webster took off his borrowed clothes and put them on a patio table near the back door of the house. Something cold touched his back. "What the – "

"It's paint, Mr. Gregg," the guide said. He held the small brush and a pot of very dark fluid up for Webster to see. "It's required that you be marked so everyone knows your part in what we are doing tonight. It will wash off."

"Oh. Okay. It's your party."

Webster stood still as the bald man painted designs on his torso and legs. The paint was cold and the brush tickled. As the paint dried, Webster felt it getting stiff against his skin. He watched the people as the bald man painted.

Everyone who was dressed wore black. Some of them had painted faces. All the naked dancers were painted with various designs. Most people had styled hair, though the dancers' hair had become wet with perspiration and hung limply as they twisted and jumped around the big fire. Webster guessed them all to be wealthy people who lived in this strange sub-division.

"You are ready," the bald man said as he stood up and put the paint and brush aside. "Come with me."

Webster followed the man to a short stage on the other side of the fire. A padded bar like a gymnast's horse rose about three feet from the center of the stage. Both ends of the stage were filled with black candles of various sizes and shapes, some elevated on bricks and some standing on the wooden boards of the stage.

"Bend over the bar, please," the bald man instructed. "Put your hands on your ankles."

Webster did as he was told. The bar, which was actually a pair of two-by-fours wrapped in foam rubber and vinyl, was warm against his cool flesh. He bent over the bar and stretched to get hold of his ankles. No sooner had he gotten his hands on his ankles than the bald man slapped his left wrist with a pair of handcuffs. He fastened the empty bracelet to his ankle.

"What the fuck is this?" Webster demanded. "Nobody said anything about handcuffs."

"It's very important that you remain in position throughout the ceremony," the bald man said. He took Webster's free arm and gently but firmly pulled it back down so that the wrist and ankle were aligned. He fastened them together with another set of handcuffs. Then he stood up and stepped off the stage.

"We are ready to begin," the bald man shouted.

The music stopped. The chattering of the guests stopped. Only the crackling of the fire and the dancing shadows cast by the flickering flames seemed to continue. Webster shifted his weight on the bar and the short chains of his handcuffs clinked.

"We are gathered here on this most sacred of nights to

give praise to his infernal majesty, Lucifer," the bald man said.

"Hail Satan!" someone shouted from the yard. The salutation was taken up by the throng. "Hail Satan!" they all cried.

"This is getting weird," Webster whispered to himself.

"Tonight we will dance, we will feast, we will engage in every carnal pleasure," the bald man said. "But first, we must affirm our loyalty to the infernal one through the Kiss of Shame. Form a single-file line at the edge of the stage and we shall begin."

And so they did. Webster remained still as the satanists filed by one at a time and kissed his anus. Some kissed quickly and moved on. Some let their lips linger; some inserted their tongues. On and on it went. Some barely touched his flesh, others pressed themselves into him. Men, women, he couldn't tell them apart by their kisses, though he could usually distinguish the difference by looking at their lower bodies between his legs.

Webster felt the blood running to his head and raised his neck. He burned inside with the need for a fix. Something in the shadows beyond the light of the candles and bonfire caught his eye. There was a figure standing there, watching the proceedings. The person was tall and dressed in a flowing black robe like that used to depict the Grim Reaper. The figure moved again and the light reflected off the pale, thin face of Luther Simmons deep within the hood of the garment. Webster stared, transfixed, unable to look away from the man.

A feeling of evil emanated from Simmons. It was something that had not been there earlier. Now, Webster felt as if he would choke on the thickness of the air, on the foul stink coming from the hooded figure. He tried to struggle but found that his limbs were too heavy to move; he couldn't even pull the chains of his handcuffs tight. Webster tried to speak, to call for help, but his mouth simply fell open and would not move.

"Have all confirmed their faith?" the bald man called. There was no answer. "Then we are ready for the arrival of our master."

The congregation began to chant in a language Webster had never heard. The robed man in front of him stepped from the shadows. His arms were crossed in front of him, his hands hidden within the sleeves. He walked slowly and gracefully around the stage. Webster followed with his eyes, finally coming to look between his own legs again. Simmons stood facing his followers. He raised his arms and the chanting immediately died.

"Tonight is my night," a voice said. Webster felt himself sagging over the padded bar. The voice came from the figure of Simmons, but it was not the voice the man had used earlier. This voice was much deeper, richer, commanding and seductive. "Tonight you will worship me openly and I will reward your devotion.

"But first, I shall seal our compact. You have given the Kiss of Shame, transferring all your purity – your innocence, your conformity to the laws of man and God – into this vessel." Simmons motioned toward Webster's buttocks. "You have shunned God in favor of me, the Usurper. I will now cleanse the vessel and destroy your transgressions against me."

Webster watched as Simmons approached him and knelt behind him. The man pushed the hood away from his face. Upside down and looking between his legs,

Webster suddenly forgot the burning in his veins, the smell coming from the man and the fact that they were being watched by dozens of creepy Satanists. As he looked into the eyes of Luther Simmons, he knew he was seeing the face of evil. The man's eyes bulged and were scarred with red veins; his flesh was like ash and he wore an expression of such malice that Webster wondered how he was able to look at the man at all.

Simmons put a hand on each of Webster's butt cheeks. The hands were like dry ice, so cold they burned. Webster moaned with the pain as the icy hot hands spread his buttocks apart. Simmons leaned forward.

"No. Please don't." From somewhere deep within, Webster was able to find the useless words.

Simmons' eyes met his and the possessed man smiled. Then he puckered his lips and shoved his face into the crevice of Webster's ass.

Webster screamed. His entire body was suddenly on fire. He tensed, his arms and legs jerking, pulling at the bindings that held him bent over the padded rail. He screamed and howled and cried but could not get away from the insistent pressure of the lips fastened to his anus.

Then his bladder and bowels let go. Piss splashed against his cheek and Webster raised his head as the rest of the stream shot forward and splashed on the ground. The lips never left his anus, but remained there and accepted the excrement as it was pushed out, as if the shit itself was the physical embodiment of the worshippers' kisses.

Webster's body tensed. His gut churned and he suddenly vomited into the puddle of piss beneath him. His abdomen clenched again and more excrement shot from his anus and into the figure attached to him.

Webster sagged over the padded bar, empty and exhausted. He felt tears running down his cheeks and was surprised he had the moisture within him to make tears.

Then Simmons pushed his tongue into Webster's body. It was like having a white-hot, writhing snake enter him. Webster tensed until he was sure his muscles would crush his bones or rip themselves apart. He howled and screamed and ... and then the warmth flooded outward from his anus and filled his body with a charge that was greater than anything he'd ever experienced with heroin, methamphetamine, crack or any other drug.

"Ah – ahhhhhh," Webster heard himself moaning. He was panting. He opened his eyes and his vision was sharp, bright, and seemed almost catlike. Objects jumped out at him with a definition he had never noticed before. The burning in his veins subsided, replaced by a warm, friendly feeling. He realized his penis was hard a moment before he ejaculated a huge amount of semen onto the stage. He moaned again and pushed his butt closer to his benefactor, burying the magic tongue deeper inside himself. "More ... " he begged. "Please. More."

The sensation went on for several more minutes. The infernal tongue explored his insides, licking and burning away all traces of the kisses left by the satanic worshippers. With every movement of the tongue, Webster felt a new rush of euphoria that was like getting a fresh injection of some wonderful new narcotic.

And then it was over. The tongue pulled out. Webster collapsed, moaning and sighing over the padded bar. The feeling of euphoria stayed with him. He heard laughing and knew it was coming from him. The bindings were taken from his wrists and ankles. He stood up and friendly hands cleaned the vomit and urine from him. The same hands led him into the group. He danced around the fire with them.

Hands pulled him to the ground, pulled him close, made him erect again and he made love to men and women, gave and received oral sex, explored soft breasts and tight orifices with his fingers and tongue and penis. He ate food, drank wine and made love some more.

Webster fell asleep eventually, the feeling of ecstasy still coursing through him. He slept hard and deep and dreamed of Luther Simmons' evil eyes and magic tongue.

When he awoke, Webster found himself in a city park. He was shaking, but it was not from the cool November air. He looked at himself and found that he was dressed again in his old ragged clothes. Simmons hadn't burned them, after all, he thought. His body screamed at him. It was the scream of withdrawal. The burning that filled his veins began at his anus. Webster searched his pockets and found that he'd been given a syringe and needle, a cigarette lighter, small spoon and plastic bottle of heroin. He cooked up a batch and shot it into his arm.

The drug didn't stop his pain. He cried and threw the syringe away. He almost threw away the bottle with the rest of the powder in it, but stopped himself. He put it back into a pocket and got to his feet. He lurched forward, not caring where he went.

Sometime later, a small white dog slipped under a gate and rushed at him, yapping and prancing. Webster groaned. Without thinking, he kicked the dog as hard as he could. The little animal sailed about thirty feet through the air, hit the ground rolling, yelped and ran away. Webster smiled. The pain within him ebbed somewhat.

"Hey you! You kicked my dog."

Webster turned and saw a man coming toward him. The man appeared to be in his early fifties, was short and thin and had gray hair. The man opened the gate and came toward Webster, an accusatory finger held before him like the gun of a tank.

"Fuck you," Webster said. He grabbed the finger and jerked it back. It snapped in his hand. A warm, soothing sensation flooded Webster's body from his anus, down his legs and up his torso, through his arms and into his brain. He sighed.

The little gray-haired man was on his knees, his broken finger still in Webster's hand. Webster released the finger and jabbed a thumb into the man's right eye. Another burst of pleasure shot through his body. He punched the man in the nose and felt another wave of euphoria.

Webster fell on the little man, pounding and poking and biting until the man stopped moving, stopped breathing. Leaving the corpse on the sidewalk, Webster went through the gate and into the man's house. He rummaged in the cabinets and refrigerator, eating handfuls of whatever looked good. He went to a bedroom and looked through the clothes, but nothing would fit him.

In the back of a closet he found a Chinese-army issue SKS rifle and a cigar box filled with ammunition. The gun held a 30-round clip. Webster loaded the clip, snapped it onto the rifle and went outside.

A red Kia was approaching, the driver slowing down to look at the bleeding man on the sidewalk. Webster raised the rifle to his shoulder, sighted and squeezed the trigger. The gun jerked and the driver of the car jumped in his seat, a new hole leaking blood from his head. The little car veered right and ran into a parked Oldsmobile.

A fresh shot of pleasure, stronger than the early ones, coursed through Webster's body. He sighed and turned his steps toward the downtown area.

Reunion

"I'm so glad you could all come today," Beverly Bauman said. "I hope no one had trouble finding the place. I know Windy Acres, Oklahoma, isn't the easiest place to find. Praise God our cars have air conditioners now. Driving out here during August could be unbearable without air conditioning. God is good."

Beverly smiled with a mouth that had never known lipstick. The mouth was part of a round, weathered face that showed more years than it owned and had never been introduced to the cosmetic artifices that would have made it look its real age. Beverly ran a hand up her forehead and over her hair, which was pulled back into a severe, deadly tight knot at the back of her head. She wore a long-sleeved, white blouse with red and blue pinstripes, and a dark blue wool skirt that fell in pleats to mid-calf. White tennis shoes were bound snugly on her large feet.

"Our house, John's and mine, is so small. We couldn't have all squeezed in there. I'm so glad our Glorious Resurrection Church let us use the sanctuary. It seems fitting we meet here. Bobby's funeral was here. This was the last place his loved ones saw what was left of him. Until now."

Beverly smiled. The fourteen people seated in the first two center pews of the small church shifted in their seats.

Some smiled politely. Others munched on homemade cookies or quietly sipped dark red punch from clear plastic cups.

"I want to tell you a story," Beverly said. "I want to tell you about our son Bobby. I think you should know something about him, considering he has become such an important part of you all."

Beverly paused. Every eye was fixed on her. She could read the expression in most faces. Only a few seemed interested in what she had to say. Some were already glazing over, as she had heard people often did in churches with uninteresting sermons. A few pairs even looked angry that she was talking about Bobby and God. Beverly looked away when she met a familiar pair of blue eyes looking back at her.

John moved silently to the doors of the sanctuary. He closed them and quietly fixed the lock. He turned to face his wife and nodded. His dark, rough hands were trembling, Beverly noted. John seemed to see her looking at them. He shoved his hands into the pockets of his navy pants.

"The Lord blessed me and John with just the one child, Bobby," Beverly said. "Oh, it was a long time ago he was given to us. I was young. Too young, really. When Bobby was delivered, the doctor said I could never have another child. But that was okay with me and John. We had one beautiful, healthy son. Praise God. We certainly did."

The people shifted a little more, chewed slowly, sipped delicately. They had no idea what they were taking into their bodies. Bodies that, in some cases, should already be as dead as Bobby's.

"In many ways, Bobby was a wonderful child," Beverly continued. "He was smart. He did well in school. He made the principal's honor roll three times in grade school and was on the honor society two semesters in junior high and one in high school. And he was good around the house. He took out the trash and milked the cows and helped with the planting and the harvest.

"It was only in church that our son was a disappointment," Beverly said. She shook her head and toyed with a button on the long striped sleeve of her blouse, taking her eyes away from her audience for a moment.

"He had no passion for the work of the Lord. It was that, finally, that caused us so much trouble. Bobby started to rebel when he became a teenager. Oh, I know that's common enough." She smiled. Only a couple of people smiled back at her. One man was already unconscious, his chin resting on his chest.

"Bobby didn't like the way we practice our faith here at the Glorious Resurrection Church," Beverly said. "He said we were too strict. He said he wanted a television. He wanted to watch that MTV channel and listen to rock and roll music and dance heathen dances. We forbade that, as is God's will.

"When Bobby turned eighteen, there was little we could do to control him. That was just one year ago today. He left home and went to that big city. Oh, I know Oklahoma City isn't such a big city, but to poor country people like us, it might as well be New York or Chicago. He went there, and only God knows all the things he did. One thing he did, though, was take up drinking. May those accursed souls of the legal moonshiners rot in Hell forever.

"Bobby had a car wreck on Interstate 40 one night, just about four months after he left home," Beverly continued. Now she took a tissue from a pocket of her skirt and dabbed at eyes that had become moist. "He was drunk, or high, or wasted, or whatever they call it. He wasn't himself. The devil had taken control of him through the drink. He was possessed by an evil spirit just as sure as if Satan himself was inside Bobby's skin.

"Me and his father never knew that Bobby had marked his driver's license to allow the state to parcel out his organs like jewels from a mine," Beverly said. She straightened herself up and wadded the tissue in her strong, farm-wife hands. More than half her audience was unconscious now. The rest were nodding or staring groggily forward.

"They took him to one of those big Oklahoma City hospitals and cut him apart and sent pieces of him all over America. Even some of his skin was taken to replace skin of people who had burned themselves," Beverly said in a hard voice.

A woman slumped forward and toppled out of the pew where she had fallen asleep. Beverly stepped away from the podium and walked carefully down the three steps from the stage and around the wide oak bench that served as an altar before the pulpit. On Sundays and Wednesdays, people crowded around the oak altar to pray.

"You have all cheated your fates, some of you have cheated death, cheated God's design for you, because of the ignorance of my son," Beverly said. "But, I am his mother, and I have to forgive him. I have to make it right. I'm his mother, after all."

"Amen," John's voice was soft and cracked as it floated from the back of the sanctuary. Beverly glanced toward him and saw the look of euphoria in his eyes. The Holy Ghost had been slow, but had come over her husband at last.

Beverly smiled and approached a middle-aged man asleep in the first pew. She took him by the chin and tilted his face up so she could look into it. "You drunkard," she accused. "You made a stone of your own liver because of the devil booze, and then they took it out and put in the young liver of my Bobby so that you could live a little longer.

"The Rapture is coming, people," Beverly shouted at the unconscious crowd, releasing the face of the liver transplant patient. "Our Lord will return and raise the bodies of the dead from their graves. But the body of our Bobby is not complete. What was his must be returned before the coming of our Lord."

"Praise the name of the Lord," said John. He had moved forward and taken a position beside Beverly.

"Yes, praise God," she said.

John's two-pound sledge hammer arced down and struck the holder of his son's liver on the crown of his head. The still, sticky, humid air of the church seemed to hold the sound of the skull cracking for a moment before letting it die with the man.

"Glory be," Beverly said as she wiped a splatter of blood from her cheek.

Suddenly, "Ringing in the Sheaves" burst forth behind her. Beverly did not turn around as the other parishioners of Glorious Resurrection Church poured from the room behind the pulpit, carrying Bobby's unearthed casket among them. She heard the box being set on the oak altar and smelled the decaying meat when the lid was opened.

"Glory be to God," John whispered as he moved to the next person, a young woman who held Bobby's beating heart within her chest. The hammer rose and fell.

"Amen," Beverly said in a quiet voice. She took the knife offered by her pastor, a short, balding man with a happy, wondrous look on his face.

Beverly knew tears were flowing from her own eyes as she sliced open the old man and lifted Bobby's liver out of the body. She handed it to her pastor and he passed it through a chain of human hands until it was placed in the coffin with the body from whence it came.

"Praise his name," Beverly said again as she moved toward her son's heart.

Summer Offspring

No Relief in Sight; State Swelters

By Aimee Tate

News-Sun Staff Writer

The National Weather Service in Norman predicted Monday that central Oklahoma will break the old record for consecutive days without rain by the end of this week.

"We've been 36 days without rain so far and there's no precipitation showing up for at least the next seven days," said meteorologist Kurt Hammond. "It looks like the summer of 2000 will go in the record books as the longest drought in state history ..."

Rash of Animal Killings Confuse Police

By Missy Abernathy

News-Sun Staff Writer

Gayle Wofford bought her pit bull, Sammy, for protection. Now, she wishes she could have protected Sammy.

"He's gone, just ripped to shreds," Wofford said between sobs.

Sammy is just the latest pet to fall victim in a rash of pet killings around the city. Police and wildlife officials speculate that the prolonged heat and drought are driving coyotes into town. They blame the wild canines for the killings.

"I've seen coyotes and dogs go crazy from the heat before," said police spokesman Sgt. Nathan Singer. "It just gets so hot, and their water holes dry up..."

Record Heat, Drought Continue to Keep People Indoors
By Aimee Tate
News-Sun Staff Writer

As Oklahoma continues to wilt under the triple-digit temperatures and record-setting drought of Summer 2000, residents are staying inside near their air conditioners.

"I haven't even been going to work," said Jim Richardson, an asphalt spreader with the city's traffic department. "It's just too hot. I'm using up all my sick leave and vacation, but that's better than dropping dead from the heat."

Finding something to keep them busy while they stay inside hasn't been a problem for most residents.

"I eat a lot of ice cream and watch Pokemon on TV," said Mattie Hayes, 4.

Ron Tibbits said he and his wife have found other ways to stay busy.

"Well, it's really hot and our air conditioner isn't very good, so we don't wear a lot of clothes," Tibbits said. "Being half naked all the time, we find things to do ..."

Water Treatment Center Up and Running Again
By Stacey Weidner
News-Sun Staff Writer

Nearly 15,000 residents were without water for about 16 hours Thursday when a rodent clogged the intake system of the city's water treatment center.

Bill Lowe, plant superintendent, said one of the 12-inch pipes that moves water through the plant became clogged early Thursday morning. That caused other pipes to back up and eventually burn out a pump in a treatment plant that was already straining to meet customers' needs during this summer's drought.

The cause of the clog turned some stomachs, Lowe said.

"It was the biggest damn rat I've ever seen," he said. "I don't know how the thing got into the pipe, but there it was, dead and wadded up against one of the filters with about 50 condoms and other pieces of solid waste.

"It was the nastiest thing I've seen in a long time," Lowe said.

Girl Missing from Local Apartment
By Missy Abernathy
News-Sun Staff Writer
The frantic cries of a mother filled the shimmering evening air outside the Rolling Oaks apartment complex late Tuesday.

Tamara Pritchett, a resident of the apartment complex, said she was playing ball with her daughter, Monique, in the apartment parking lot when the ball rolled into a storm drain. Tamara Pritchett went to find a friend to see if he could get the ball out of the drain. When she came back, her 6-year-old daughter was gone ...

Report Says Not to Anticipate Spring 2001 Baby Boom

From Associated Press Reports

A recent Guff Company survey has found that condom sales have risen by 38 percent in the states affected by this summer's unseasonably high temperatures.

"When people stay indoors because of the heat, they are more likely to use condoms or some other form of birth control," said Joyce Horn, professor of sociology at North Central Oklahoma College. "It seems couples are more open to the idea of starting a family when it's cold outside. When it's hot, they're just looking for pleasure ..."

Two Boys Missing
By Missy Abernathy
News-Sun Staff Writer

Tommy Powell and David Denton, both 12, often rode their bikes on N 19 Street. Neighbors say the boys would also build ramps to jump the storm ditch that ran beside the road, or crawl through the culvert where the ditch passes under E Ash Avenue.

Saturday afternoon, the boys' bicycles were found near the north end of the culvert, but the boys haven't been seen since late that morning.

"We think they might have gone in there and then crawled into the smaller tunnel that empties into this ditch," said police spokesman Sgt. Nathan Singer. "So far, we haven't found them ..."

Murder Suspect Released; Authorities Apologize
By Kevin O'Connor
News-Sun Staff Writer

Dale Washington was released from the city jail Wednesday morning. District Attorney Kathy Maddox said the two first-degree murder charges against Washington have been dropped.

"It has been determined by forensic investigators that the bite marks on the two victims could not have been made by Mr. Washington," Maddox said in a news conference Wednesday. "DNA evidence confirms that Mr. Washington's wife and son were the victims of some kind of animal attack."

Washington, who has become known as "Ratman," spent 21 days in the county jail, accused of murdering his wife and their infant son in their apartment. Police reports state that, upon his arrest, Washington was hysterical. The report says he was holding the bloody body of his three-month-old son. There were large bite marks on the child's body and blood on Washington's mouth.

"I told them I didn't do it," Washington said during Wednesday's news conference. "I was just trying to give my son CPR. It was the rats that killed him ..."

Homeless Man Found Mauled to Death
By Stacey Weidner
News-Sun Staff Writer

City police and state wildlife officials are examining the death of a homeless man found in a Burlington-Northern railroad switching station Friday afternoon. Police reports say the man was apparently mauled and partially devoured by some kind of animal.

"We don't know what kind of animal it was," said Gayleen Babbs, a spokeswoman with the state Wildlife Department. "We do know that there was more than one animal involved."

A report from the state medical examiner says the unidentified man appeared to have been overwhelmed while intoxicated and asleep.

"His body is covered in bites of varying size from head to foot," Babbs said. She added that the bite marks do not match any known animal ...

City Plagued by Animal Attacks
From Staff Reports

What began with the killing of outdoor pets has become much more serious. Police and wildlife officials have linked the pet slayings to the deaths of 12 people in the metro area, and suspect the disappearance of several others – mostly children – to also be the responsibility of wild animals.

"The bite marks on most of the pets that have been killed recently match the patterns we've found on several humans that have also been killed and partially eaten," said department of wildlife spokeswoman Gayleen Babbs. "Unfortunately, we still can't confirm what kind of animals we're dealing with. All we know is that there are a lot of them and that they attack at night."

Police officials say they believe the animals are living in the city's sewer system by day and coming out in search of food by night.

"From what we've been able to learn from when people are reported missing and from lab reports to determine time of death, it does appear that the animals kill at night," said Sgt. Nathan Singer, a police spokesman.

Singer said he has asked the governor to provide National Guard assistance to create a task force to venture into the sewer system to find the animals responsible for the deaths.

"Based on what we've learned from lab reports, we think there are just too many of them for our department to handle," Singer said.

A spokeswoman for the governor said a decision on whether or not to activate the National Guard should be made public later today. Even if approved, it could be two to three days before troops enter the city's sewer system.

In the meantime, residents are urged to remain indoors after dark and to keep their doors and windows locked. City Manager Mike Hughes said he plans to call an emergency meeting of the city council Monday to discuss further action.

"I will ask the council to pass a mandatory curfew on the city," Hughes said. "I don't think anyone should be allowed out after dark until we can ..."

Resident Kills Rat-like Creature
By Kevin O'Conner and Missy Abernathy
News-Sun Staff Writers

Mildred Williams, 68, knew it was no ordinary burglars scratching at her window late Sunday night. What she didn't know was that she would be the first resident to survive an attack by the strange creatures that have been stalking the city by night.

"I grew up on a farm out by Tuttle," Williams said. "I've drowned skunks, shot coyotes and trapped coons. But I ain't never saw nothing like those varmints last night."

The "varmints" Williams saw numbered about two dozen, she said. Six of them weren't able to leave her home on the city's north side.

"I blasted the hell out of them," said the grandmother of four.

But the question remains: What are the strange animals? The shotgun-riddled bodies of the six animals shot by Williams have been taken for examination by state wildlife officials. Williams said she's never seen anything like the animals.

"They look like little kids, except they're rats," she said. "They walk on their hind legs, but are about as tall as my youngest granddaughter. She's a pre-schooler. They're covered in hair and have a face and tail just like a rat. Damned if I know what they are, but they come messing around here again, I'll sure as hell shoot some more of them ..."

Police Admit Knowing of Rat-like Creatures
By Stacey Weidner
News-Sun Staff Writer

Local police admitted late Monday that they have known for over a week that the animal attacks plaguing the city have been from some kind of rat-like creature.

"We have known, but we chose not to make that information public," said police spokesman Sgt. Nathan Singer. "We felt it would incite a public panic."

Now it seems panic is mixed with outrage as many residents work to turn their homes into fortified sanctuaries. Local lumberyards are being hard pressed to meet the needs of customers wanting material to board-up their doors and windows. Grocery store shelves are also under attack from customers stocking up as if for a siege. Many residents say they are closing their homes against the rat creatures and the police.

"I can't believe they would withhold that kind of information," said Karen Dandridge as she filled a grocery basket with supplies. "Who can you trust? My husband is at the sporting goods store right now buying ammunition. We'll shoot anything that comes scratching, gnawing or clawing at our house ..."

National Guard Enters City
By Kevin O'Connor
News-Sun Staff Writer

The Oklahoma National Guard came into town late Monday night and are expected to enter the city's vast sewer system at around 3 p.m. today.

"We're studying blueprints of the system now," said Lt. Dan Coffey.

Coffey said his troops will be armed primarily with flame-throwers and handguns. Each guard will be equipped with lighted helmets and orders to kill.

"This isn't a rescue mission," Coffey said. "We're going in to kill them."

That has sparked a new controversy with animal rights activists who have descended on the city since it was learned the National Guard would be coming to town.

"We don't know exactly what these animals are," said Michael Hart of People Against Animal Cruelty (PAAC). "We have no right to go into their homes and exterminate them."

Protesters and residents have already clashed in several skirmishes around city hall, forcing the governor to activate even more National Guard troops to keep the peace and patrol city streets.

"I can't believe these whack-o people," said Oliver Haslett, a resident who came to city hall to get a building permit and was confronted by several PAAC members. "What do they think is going on here? These animals are breaking into our homes and killing us. I'd like to see how many of these freaks stay out here carrying their signs after dark ..."

DNA Experts Say Rat-Creatures Are Half Human
By Aimee Tate and Missy Abernathy
News-Sun Staff Writers

State forensics experts released a report late Tuesday saying the vicious animals preying on the city are half human and half rat.

"We didn't dare to believe it at first, although when you see them, it's pretty obvious," said Cindy Kline, a forensics expert with the Oklahoma State Bureau of Investigation. "They have several human characteristics, such as walking on their hind legs and, we believe, the ability to use tools. They have the incisors common to rats, but their back teeth are very similar to human molars."

Kline could only speculate on how the creatures came into existence.

"The only theory we have is that normal rats living in the sewer were exposed to condoms flushed down city toilets," Kline said. "Ordinarily, semen would die long before it ever got that far into the sewer. However, because of the long heat wave and lack of rain to really flush the sewers out, it's possible the sperm in the condoms didn't die and somehow entered the body of a few female rats. One female rat can spawn dozens of offspring in a very short time, so it's easy to see how we could have such a high population of these things very quickly.

"From there, it's really just a logical evolution to the animals we're dealing with now," she said.

City leaders were skeptical of the report.

"It sounds like some kind of sick Stephen King-type trash to me," said City Manager Mike Hughes.

National Guard troops had already entered the city's sewer system when the report was released. Operation Sewer Sweep commander, Lt. Dan Coffey, was contacted via radio from a command post established at city hall. He wasn't impressed by the report.

"I don't care if it's a race of midgets living down here," Coffey said from the sewer. "They're killing Oklahomans and my orders are to kill them. That's what I plan to do."

Residents are shocked by the DNA report, but most still support the National Guard effort to exterminate the creatures, regardless of their origin ...

PAAC Protesters Killed, Missing; National Guard Suffers Casualties

From Staff Reports

Sixteen members of People Against Animal Cruelty (PAAC) were found mauled and partially eaten around city hall Wednesday morning. The remaining 12 members of the group, who had come to town to protest National Guard plans to kill the animals preying on the city, cannot be found, police say.

"It's pretty obvious the rat-creatures got to the protesters," said police spokesman Sgt. Nathan Singer.

"The evidence is all there, just like in the other cases. We ordered them off the street, even escorted many of them to their hotel, but we got a report a few hours later from the mayor saying they had come back to city hall and were marching again."

The animal-rights activists weren't the only ones to suffer casualties.

Seven National Guard soldiers are currently in All Saints Hospital being treated for bites sustained in the city's sewer system Tuesday night. Three others are reportedly dead, killed fighting the sewer-dwelling animals that some experts say are half-human ...

National Guard Says Mission a Success
By Stacey Weidner
News-Sun Staff Writer

Operation Sewer Sweep was a complete success, according to commander Lt. Dan Coffey.

"We spent about 36 hours down there and killed probably over 1,500 of the beasts," Coffey said. "We killed all of them we saw and explored every route shown on city blueprints. They had nowhere to go. We got them all."

Not all his troops share the commander's confidence or brashness. One private who asked to remain anonymous said he had never been as scared as he was in the city sewer system.

"There were thousands of those red eyes staring at us, just about waist-high," the soldier said. "We just turned loose with the flame-throwers and side-arms, but those things weren't scared. They came right at us."

National Guard casualties total 23 dead, 52 injured and nine missing, Coffey said.

"The loss of my men is tragic, but considering that it was one hell of a tough mission down there, I still say it was a total success ..."

From the News-Sun Editorial Page

The following letter was received in our office on Nov. 1. At first, we were inclined to believe it was a sick hoax. Still, we turned it over to the police for investigation. They, in turn, sent it to the state Bureau of Investigation. Cindy Kline, the DNA expert who proposed the theory that the rat-like creatures that preyed on our city during the late summer months were half human, said the stains on the original letter were made by semen from a creature such as she had examined. She said she believes the following letter is authentic. In the interest of public safety, we have chosen to print the letter.

– Lyndon Everson, executive editor of the News-Sun

Dear Readers,

You have destroyed hundreds of my brothers and sisters, but you failed to kill just as many. We won't forget your efforts to exterminate us. We are busy now, as you can see from the stains on this paper. You will see us again.

Woman Trains Mutant to Speak, Tries to Protect Pet from Government

By Louis DeValcourt

Associated Press Writer

PHOENIX – A local woman has a very unusual pet. The creature stands nearly four feet tall, is covered in long gray hair and has all the facial characteristics of a common rat. However, it walks on its rear legs and has learned to speak a few words in harsh, broken English.

"I found him beside the road when he was just a baby," said Sharilyn Hubbard, who lives in a small house she built in the desert just outside Phoenix. "He was no bigger than my hand just six months ago."

Keeping the animal, named Harvey, is forcing Hubbard into the fight of her life. Government officials claim Harvey is an escaped half human, half rat creature like the ones that reportedly killed numerous people in central Oklahoma last year. Hubbard says she has already been ordered to turn the animal over to authorities, but so far she has refused to comply. She has turned to the public, hoping for support.

That may be hard to get, however. Since going public with her cause, FBI officials have released a video they say Hubbard has been selling on the Internet. The video shows Hubbard copulating with her pet ...

Wandering John

The man's feet hurt him. His shoes were old, each with worn-down heels and holes under the balls of his feet. A long time ago, when the original owner had them, the shoes were shiny brown leather. Now, they were filthy, smudged with mud, garbage and animal waste, with untied laces flopping softly on the concrete sidewalk as the man shuffled through the dark neighborhood. A long pea-green overcoat flapped against his shins as he walked, making a soft patting sound.

He wasn't sure what city he was in today. After so many, many years, they all came to look about the same. It was a fairly large city, though nothing like New York. The man was pretty sure he was in Oklahoma, so the city was probably either Tulsa or Oklahoma City. He glanced around and found a billboard advertising tickets to Oklahoma City Blazers hockey games. It really didn't matter.

He spat toward the street gutter, not bothering to watch the twisting mass of stuff he ejected from his body.

He was very tired.

The man called himself Wandering John. John might even be his real name; he couldn't remember. All he knew for sure was that he heard the call telling him which direction to go, where his services were needed, and he followed it. Today he was moving west.

He turned a corner and spat again. Behind him, a cat yowled, raced past him and attacked the curb where John's spit landed. John didn't care. There would be more. All the cats in the world couldn't match him.

God had called him to this duty. John didn't especially like it, but he couldn't argue. He simply had to do what he was told to do. It wasn't as if he really had a choice in the matter – he'd awakened one morning after a night of sleeping in a Washington, D.C., gutter and discovered his ability. No fanfare. No voice from Heaven. Just the need to spit and keep moving.

His mouth filled again. The taste was old, like mildew growing on decayed wood in the basement of an abandoned house. He could feel sharp little claws scraping at his tongue and the backs of his teeth. John spat between a pair of overflowing trash Dumpsters.

He moved on, his long, stained green coat flapping around him, his black stocking cap pulled over his ears. He was still cold. He pulled a gloved hand from his coat pocket and wiped a streak of stale-smelling saliva from his whiskery chin. A car rolled by in the street to his left; he could hear the boom of rap music coming from the vehicle.

John felt more of his gift pushing through the glands under his tongue. He heaved a weary sigh, sucked his tongue to work up some lubricating saliva, and spat at the concrete foundation of an old warehouse.

In the faint glow of a streetlight he could see the little blob of fetuses writhing on the sidewalk – tiny blind mouse eyes looking from side to side while delicate claws tore at the cold air. His saliva glistened against the hairless pink skin of the four infant rodents.

Only four, he thought. He hadn't waited long enough before spitting. Oh well. There would be more. Always more. He moved on, ignoring the sound of soft cat feet rushing toward his gift.

John held the next litter until his cheeks puffed, and when he spat he couldn't muster the force to project his babies far; one rolled down his chin and crunched under the hole in the bottom of his right shoe.

Wandering John wiped his lips, shook his head, and kept walking. Always more, he thought. Always more.

As the sky began to turn pink in the east, John left the streets and followed a pair of train tracks to a bridge over a little river. He turned right and walked west along the riverbank. He spat when he needed to, paying no mind to the sound of cats behind him. When the horizon was grey behind him, John settled himself into the shadowy space under a highway bridge spanning the river and slept, lulled to sleep by the sound of morning traffic passing over his head.

* * *

John felt the shadows changing on his face as the sun slipped behind the western edge of the Oklahoma City skyline. The musty aftertaste of rodent birth was still in his mouth. Without opening his eyes, John turned his head and spat. Then he realized he did not feel the wet writhing of tiny bodies around his hands or on his chest. He slowly opened his eyes.

A small woman squatted before him. She wore ragged tennis shoes, limp socks, filthy dark blue slacks with lighter vertical stripes and a yellow T-shirt. Her black hair had strands of grey and hung around her browned face in oily mats. Large eyeglasses weighed heavily on her nose and magnified her brown eyes so that they looked twice their real size.

"Who are you?" John asked. His mouth suddenly filled. He pursed his lips and glared at the intruding woman. There was nothing else to do. John turned his head and spat.

"Whutcha gonna do widdum?" the woman asked in a voice that sounded as if it were pushed through a filter of mucus before being allowed to leave her body. John followed her eyes in the direction in which he'd spat. Five small pink bodies squirmed on the shadow-dark ground.

"What?" he asked.

"Can I have 'em?"

John stared at the woman and didn't answer. She looked away, then shot a thin arm forward and grasped the tiny mice in a dirty fist.

"Don't do – " John spoke too late. The dirty little woman popped all five wriggling rodents into her mouth. He heard the frail skeletons crunch between her teeth. "Why did you do that?"

"Hungry," she said, still chewing.

John looked away and got slowly to his feet. Sleeping outside did not agree with him anymore. His knees were stiff and his back ached. He glanced at the woman, still squatting and munching, and walked away from her.

He went down the earthen slope to the river and sank back to his knees. With cupped hands, he splashed cool water on his face, then rinsed out his mouth. When he straightened, the woman was standing beside him.

"You do that all the time?" she asked. "You was doin' it while you was asleep. They's fallin' outta yer mouth and rollin' off yer chest."

"I suppose you ate those, too."

"Course I did. I tol' ya I'm hungry. Ya gonna have any more?"

"That's disgusting."

"Yer the one spittin' mice babies, mister. Don't tell me my business. I gotta eat. You don't never eat none of 'em yerself?"

"No."

"Why not?"

"Who are you? Why are you bothering me?" John asked.

"Names Andrea. Whut's yers?"

"John. Why are you bothering me?"

"I just found ya laying unner the bridge there. I sleep there sometimes, myself. Ya had all those things aroun' ya, and I was hungry, so I et 'em."

"Some people beg, or find food in restaurant trash bins," John said.

"I've done all that. I got sicker'n a dog once from eatin' fried chicken what had been throwed out."

"You'd rather eat the fetuses of mice? Raw and alive?"

"Why not?"

John shook his head and walked away again. His mouth filled. He turned his head, then turned the other way and spat into the river.

"Why'd you do that? I'm still hungry. I ain't goin' in after 'em." The woman hurried to his side.

"Where does this river go?" John asked. He pointed to the west along the bank of the river.

"I dunno. Yukon mebbe. El Reno."

"Are those big towns?"

"I dunno. Never been. I saw 'em on the TV news in the shelter downtown. This is the South Canadian River."

"I have to go west. I'll follow the river," John said.

"Whutcha mean, you gotta go west? Who said?"

"God."

"God don't talk to nobody."

"Whatever." John kept walking, keeping the river on his left. Andrea stayed on his right, nearly jogging to keep pace with him.

"I'll come widchu."

"You don't have to."

"I wanna."

"I'd rather you didn't."

"I might let ya fuck me."

John spat into the river again. A fish rose to the surface and swallowed the two pink bodies as soon as they hit the water. "No thanks," John said.

"You a fag?"

"I've gotten used to being alone."

"You ain't gotta be alone."

"I don't mind."

"I'm comin' with ya unless you push me in the river or sumpin."

John glanced over at her and considered grabbing her and throwing her into the water and continuing to walk. But he wasn't sure yet. He sighed and shook his head. "I won't let you slow me down. I won't wait on you."

"Fine. You won't need to."

"I have to pee." John looked back and decided he was far enough away from where the highway went over the river. He reached for the zipper of his pants, then stopped. Andrea was watching him. "Turn away, please."

"Why? You ain't got nuttin I ain't see b'fore. 'Sides that, if I'm gonna be handlin' it later, I might as well see it now."

John turned away, opened his pants and pulled himself out. He couldn't help a slight moan as the arc of piss splashed into the river. He tucked himself back in and turned around to find Andrea with her blue-striped slacks around her ankles as she squatted on the ground, a puddle forming beneath her and running past one sneaker toward the river. John stepped over the stream and walked on. Andrea caught up with him a moment later.

"Ya ain't the only one gotta piss ever mornin'," she said.

John spat in the river again.

"You keep spittin' those things in the river and ya ain't gonna get no pussy offa me," Andrea said.

John ignored her.

"Why'd God tell ya to go west?"

"To deliver mice."

"Ain't they got no mice out west?"

"I don't question him. I just go."

"You some kinda Johnny Appleseed, plantin' mice all over the place?"

"The ones that don't get eaten by cats, fish or crazy women."

"I ain't crazy. They put me in a loony bin once, my worthless kids did, but the doctors hadda lemme out 'cause I ain't crazy."

"How long do you plan to stay with me?"

"I dunno. I like you. You didn't throw me in the river. How long ya been spittin' mice babies?"

"A long time."

"How'd it start?"

"I don't know. I just woke up doing it one morning."

"You livin' on the street when it happened?"

"Yes."

"That's gotta be a bitch."

"Yes."

"You don't talk much."

"Nope."

"I don't mind. I talk enough fer both of us."

John grunted. There was a shallow bend in the river, which at this point was choked with old tires, twisted, rusted pieces of metal and other debris. He spat into the murky water and pulled a dented can of tuna from a jacket pocket. He opened the can and tossed the lid into the river with the rest of the human junk.

"Whatcha got?"

"Tuna."

"Smells like cat food. You gonna share? If yer not, ya better gimme some more a them mice babies."

Reluctantly, John held the can toward her. Andrea scooped out half the contents with her dirty hand. John scooped out the rest, tossed the can aside and ate the pungent fish from his fingers.

They walked, following the river. John spat into the water when he needed to and drank from it when the water looked clean enough. Andrea talked incessantly, mostly complaining about her children and how they'd always mistreated her until they put her in the loony bin.

"If yer on a mission to put mice babies ever'where, why come ya keep spittin' 'em in the river? Won't that make God mad?"

"There's always more," John said. "If I don't spit these

in the river, you'll just eat them. That would probably make God madder. The fish don't know any better."

They continued walking. John's stomach rumbled. He knew he had another can of tuna and a bag of animal crackers – both over two months out of date – in his coat pockets, but he didn't want to share them with his unwanted companion. He waited and walked. Andrea hurried along beside him, chattering. Sometime after midnight they left the outskirts of Oklahoma City. The water caught the reflection of the moon and stars; the sound of nocturnal animals interrupted Andrea every once in a while.

"You wanna fuck now?"

"No," John answered.

"I ain't been with a man this long without fuckin' him since I got outta the loony bin. You sure you don't wanna fuck me now? I'm ready for it."

"I'm sure."

"You'll fuck me later, though. Right?"

"I doubt it."

"You won't gimme no more a those mice babies and now you ain't gonna gimme no dick? You're a bastard."

"I guess."

John pulled the bag of animal cookies from his pocket and tore it open. He held the bag toward Andrea, hoping she'd fill her mouth and be quiet for a while. She looked at the bag for a moment, then crinkled her nose and shook her head. John began eating. Andrea continued talking, this time about her former husband. They walked.

They stopped a couple more times during the night, when John absolutely could not hold his waste any longer. He felt fortunate that Andrea didn't look at him as he squatted in some tall weeds to move his bowels, but she kept talking just the same, even when she decided at the last minute that she had to go, too. She squatted in the weeds a couple of yards away, pausing her chatter only long enough to scrunch up her face a couple of times. John tossed her a couple of napkins he'd taken from a McDonald's restaurant to wipe with. When she was finished, she straightened, pulled up her slacks and kicked dirt over her shit. Scowling, John did the same. He washed his hands in the river; Andrea did not wash. John decided there was no way he was allowing her to put her hands into his other tuna can.

They walked. John spat. The stars began to dim. John knew the dawn was coming. He began looking for a suitable place to pass the daylight hours. He hoped making camp would cause Andrea to shut up for a while.

After a half-hour he found a dilapidated lean-to made of rotting two-by-fours with a corrugated tin roof. The sagging structure was about twenty-five yards from the riverbank and had a floor of straw. John guessed it had once been used to keep bales of hay dry.

"I'm going to sleep here for a while," he announced.

"Sounds fine by me," Andrea agreed. "We gonna eat first?"

John frowned and looked away. He was hungry and her hands were dirty. He didn't want to share his tuna. As it was, it was the last bit of food he had and he didn't know when he'd find more.

"If I give you some mice, the last can of tuna I have in my pocket is mine. Understand?"

"Sure, I unnerstand. No problem."

John looked away from her, sucked his tongue a few

times and felt the rodents come squirming from his glands. He spat into the straw. Andrea fell on the pink morsels like a child on candy from a piñata. John spat more fetuses in her direction, then went outside to sit under a tree behind the lean-to. He opened his tuna can and ate.

When he returned to the shelter of the rusted roof he found Andrea lying on the straw, naked. She was touching herself, one hand on her small breast, the other rubbing between her legs. The sound told John she already was well lubricated.

"Tell me you don't want somma this," she said.

John sighed. He felt a stirring in his groin despite himself. He looked at Andrea more closely. He wondered how long it had been since she'd shaved her legs – it looked like weeks, or even months. He was glad he couldn't see under her arms. Grime filled the creases in the flesh beneath her breasts. Her glasses were off, folded on top of the pile of clothing not far from her head. She moaned.

"Please John?"

John shrugged off his long green coat, pushed off his shoes and let his pants fall to his ankles, leaving his shirt on. He stepped out of his pants and knelt between the woman's legs. She didn't smell good. He took his penis in his hand and pulled a few times until it was stiff enough to take care of business, then he lowered himself and pushed into her. He slid in easily. Andrea gasped, then moaned and wrapped her hairy legs around his.

John pumped steadily. He soon forgot about the woman's rank smell, her dirty body, matted hair and ceaseless talk. She was simply a woman who wanted him, and it had been so long since he'd experienced this kind of intimacy with anyone. He let himself enjoy it, not allowing himself to think about what would happen later.

As he finished, it was like his entire insides were concentrated in his groin and exploding through his penis. He shoved deep, tensed once, twice, a third time, felt himself throbbing and spitting as something that was not a grunt, not a scream came from his mouth. Beneath him, Andrea tightened her grip on him and dug her fingers into his arms, her lips pulled back in a feline snarl as she gasped and grunted.

John sagged forward, barely holding all his weight off the small woman. Her grip loosened and she slid her hands up to his head and pulled him closer, kissing him and then pushing his face against her shoulder. She nuzzled him with her cheek, something like a purr coming from her throat.

"John?"

"Umm?"

"Aint it funny how people like us come together? Weird people? You know yer weird, what with the mouse thing and all."

"Umm-hmm."

She continued nuzzling him. "I got my own problems. I guess there was a reason my kids put me in that loony bin. I ain't esactly normal."

"I know."

"Nah. Ya don't know, John. Ya can't know."

"Umm."

"You ain't the only one what's strange. You remember that, John."

"Umm-hmm."

John pushed himself off her, pulled on his pants and

reached for his overcoat. Andrea made no move to dress. John covered them both with the coat and settled down to sleep. He was out before the first light came into the sky.

* * *

John awoke to the sensation of a small, rough tongue licking his chin. He snorted and tried to turn away. Something warm moved with him. Just as he realized there was an unusual weight on his chest, something hairy pushed itself between his lips. John sat up, his eyes popping open as his hands caught the cat that was trying to get a snack from his mouth.

Judging from the light, John guessed it to be mid-afternoon. He looked at the cat, a dark-haired female streaked with grey. The animal looked back at him, not squirming to get away, not clawing at him, simply looking. She began to purr.

"That'll do you no good," John said. He pushed the coat off his lap with one hand, keeping the cat in the other. "I'm sorry, Andrea. I really am."

He pulled the coat up and covered the cat, released her and rolled the coat into a ball, trapping the feline within it. The cat squalled and fought, but John held the coat in a tight bundle. He picked it up, still holding it firmly together, and walked toward the river.

"The mice are just bait, you see," he said to the bulging coat. "My mission is not to spread mice. It's to find abominations like you and destroy them. I'm sorry, Andrea. I shouldn't have made love to you. That wasn't fair of me. I knew what it would do to you."

He knelt beside the river, took a deep breath and plunged the coat into the cool water. The cat inside became more frantic. One paw escaped the coat and tiny claws dug into John's arm. He didn't flinch, only tightened his grip and hardened his resolve. After a couple of minutes, the struggle was over. John waited a couple more minutes before lifting the dripping coat from the water. He unrolled it and looked at the wet, dead animal. Andrea's cat eyes were wide open and staring. Water leaked from her parted lips.

John turned his head and spat mice into the river.

Warren Pepper's Victory Choir

"You're not afraid of me, are you Derrick?"

"No sir, Mr. Baker, I'm not." The tall orderly had skin so black it looked as though somebody had poured used-up motor oil over his heavily-muscled body. His smile, like the whites of his eyes and the bleached clothes he wore, seemed to glow with a holy fire against the ebony of his flesh. "Why should I be afraid of you?"

"You know what I am," Tim Baker answered.

"I know what you was," Derrick corrected. He lifted a spoonful of oatmeal to the mouth of his patient.

"But you're not afraid of me. You've heard the doctors talk about me. You're thinking about it right now. I can see it in your eyes."

"Well now, Mr. Baker, I ain't one to deny I've heard such talk." Derrick flashed a gleaming smile. "What's past is past, though."

"But you're still not afraid. Most people, when they come in here and see me like this--" Tim glanced down at his body, which was confined in the bed of the mental ward with several canvas straps. "They're afraid."

"What do I have to be afraid of?" Derrick asked as he scooped more oatmeal into Tim's mouth. "You're trussed up like a Christmas turkey."

"You know what I did."

111

"Yes, I know. But you ain't like that no more. That's why you're here. You're learning that you can't be like that no more."

Tim Baker laughed. Flecks of mushy oatmeal sprayed from his mouth. Derrick's smile never faltered as he wiped the gray flecks from his own arms and shirt and then from the patient's laughing mouth.

"What makes you think I want to change, Derrick? Maybe I like what I am. Maybe I need to...need to do it. Maybe that's why they keep me like this -- trussed up, as you put it."

"No sir, you don't like it," Derrick said. "You don't. It ain't natural. You know that. Besides, you ain't done nothing bad in a long, long time. I heard the doctors saying the other day that you're doing real good, 'cept for some occasional crazy talk that still worries them."

"You're right about one thing. It ain't natural. It's supernatural."

Derrick chuckled deep in his thick chest. He spooned more oatmeal toward Tim's mouth. The cereal had been warm when they began breakfast but it had ceased to steam some time ago. Now it looked like so much congealed brain pudding.

"Do you believe in Hell, Derrick?"

"Yes sir, I do. Not that I'm worried about it." He winked. "My momma saw to it all her children were saved in the church. Someday, hopefully not too soon, you understand, but someday I'll be going to Heaven."

Tim roared with laughter until he finally choked on the glob of cereal in his mouth. "You're crazy, Derrick. Plumb fucking crazy. There's no Heaven. There's only Hell. I know. I can hear the people in there screaming."

"Now, Mr. Baker, we don't want to hear that. You know I'll have to give you a pill if you keep talking about that. I always do. Doctor's orders. You'll get yourself all worked up and try to hurt yourself again. Don't you want to get to where you can do without these straps?"

"The pill," Tim said, smiling sadly. "Do you think your fucking pill helps? It just makes the screaming louder. The only difference is that I can't tell you about it because I can't move my mouth. It just hangs open with slobber dripping out. That makes the pretty little nurses want to gag, doesn't it?"

"Well now, I don't know nothing about that," Derrick said, but Tim knew it was a lie.

"How long you been working here at the loony bin, Derrick?"

"I've been here a month and three days now."

"Who's your favorite patient?"

"You are, of course, Mr. Baker." Derrick smiled and Tim laughed a sane, friendly laugh. Suddenly the laugh broke into a sob and his face became lined and tense, making him look twenty years older than he really was.

"Please Derrick, tell me you're really my friend. A real friend," he begged in a hoarse whisper. "I haven't had a real friend in so long. These doctors and nurses don't like me. I'm like an animal in a cage to them...something they examine and nod over while they write their little notes. I didn't want to do what I did. Won't anybody ever look at me and not think about that?"

"Of course I'm your friend, Mr. Baker," Derrick answered. "You don't need to fuss over that. I'll always be your friend. As for what you did, that was before I met you, so I don't think much about it. You're just a man I'm

113

trying to help, same as Mr. Hopkins in the room next door."

"Sam Hopkins is just a drooling retard."

"Now, Mr. Baker, we don't need to talk that way."

"I'm tired of being here, Derrick. So tired. I want to go outside. I want to feel the sun and smell the starlight and roll in the grass. And I want a woman. Did you know I've never had one?"

"If you want to take a nap, Mr. Baker, I can probably get you something to help you sleep," Derrick offered. "You look like you could use a good nap."

"No, Derrick, no. That's not what I need. I'm tired in my soul, not in my body. Do you have time? Time to listen to me? I want to talk. I want to tell you what happened. I like you, Derrick. You're not like those doctors who won't believe anything or the nurses who act like they'll get leprosy from coming in the room with me. Please listen to me."

Derrick glanced toward the door of the sterile little room. Through a small, square glass window with wire-mesh reinforcement he could see the round face of a clock mounted on the wall of the corridor outside the room. It was ten minutes before 8 a.m. "My shift's about over, Mr. Baker," Derrick began, then stopped. He had never seen a man's face look as earnest as Tim Baker's did at that moment. "I reckon I can stay a little while, though."

"Thank you, Derrick. Thank you." Tim's head fell back onto his pillow. He smiled wanly. "I'd shake your hand if I could get mine out of these straps."

"It's the thought that counts, Mr. Baker."

Tim laughed softly. "You should have been a damn politician, Derrick. You always know just what to say without saying anything."

Derrick chuckled again. "What is it you want to tell me, Mr. Baker?"

"I want to tell you about the ears. And about Warren Pepper and his root cellar. That's where it all started, you know. Well, sort of. I guess it really started in Vietnam. Not for me, though. For me it started in Warren Pepper's root cellar. That was about five years after he died."

"Warren Pepper got sent to the war in Vietnam. I remember the day he left. Everybody in the neighborhood turned out to see him off. His dad was crying and cussing. His dad said Vietnam wasn't a war, it was a goddamn excuse for Jack Kennedy to kill young American boys so he could have more American women. I didn't know what the hell he meant...or even who Jack Kennedy was back then. I was only six and JFK had been dead for a couple of years already. I just remember it because it was said by a grown man who was crying like a little kid."

"I guess nobody expected Warren Pepper to come home from the war. A lot of boys didn't. But Warren did. He came home. His mom had a big party that day. I remember seeing Warren at the party for a while -- he was about twelve years older than me. He'd been gone for just over a year. I didn't know that one year was too short a time to be in the army. I heard my mom and dad talking about Warren Pepper being "Section Eight" but I didn't know what it meant. Anyway, Warren didn't stay at the party long. He left. Went out the back door and wasn't seen again that day."

"His mom and dad weren't seen too much after that, either. His dad went to work at the refinery in the mornings and came home in the evenings. His mom went to the grocery store every Saturday. Nobody ever saw Warren Pepper, though. I remember his mom and dad got to looking real old real fast."

"And then one day Warren Pepper's dad came running out of the house with a red cloth over his ear. But the cloth wasn't really red. It was soaked in blood. Me and David, my best friend, were riding our bikes when old man Pepper came running out with that rag to his head. It was dripping blood and he was screaming 'He's killing us! He's killing us!' Then Mrs. Pepper came out, too, and she wasn't holding a rag. Her right ear was gone. Just gone."

"Warren came to the door then. He looked sick. He was real skinny, like those concentration camp pictures, and his eyes glowed like little flashlights. He had a big butcher knife in one hand."

"'You sent me there,' Warren screamed. 'You helped them do this to me. Now I'll be able to hear you screaming in Hell.' Then he closed the door. Some other neighbors had come out and were trying to help his mom and dad. We could hear sirens coming."

"Then there was a blast from inside the house. Warren Pepper blew his brains out with his dad's double-barreled shotgun. Both barrels in his mouth. He was a mess. He--"

"You saw him?" Derrick interrupted.

"Oh yeah, I saw him. But not that day. Like I said, he'd been dead for about five years when I saw him."

"Now, Mr. Baker, are you--"

"Let me finish, Derrick. You'll see. Then you can go home and see your wife and tell her the truth about the crazy man at work who's strapped in his bed. You've told her about me and what the doctors have said, haven't you?"

"I ... I guess I've mentioned you," Derrick admitted.

"It's okay. People have to talk. It's what keeps us sane, huh?" He grinned.

"Go on with your story, Mr. Baker. What happened after Warren Pepper shot himself."

"His parents moved away. He'd cut an ear off both of them. I never saw them again after that time they came running out of the house with blood all over them.

"Years went by. The Pepper house stood empty. It wasn't a big house; just a one-story, three-bedroom house in a neighborhood where all the homes looked pretty much alike. Turns out Warren Pepper's grandfather actually owned the house and had been letting Mrs. Pepper and her husband buy it from him a little at a time. He tried to sell it once after that stuff happened. There was a sign in the yard for a while, but nobody would buy it. That was about the same time the refinery closed, so nobody was buying houses then."

"Like I said, years went by. I was thirteen when me and David decided to break into the root cellar of the old Pepper house. It was a mound of earth with a warped wooden door that had been painted red. Most of the paint was coming off and the whole top of the cellar was covered in vines from a vegetable garden that grew wild in the backyard every year. We had to cut some of the vines away just to get to the door.

"You know what a cellar smells like, don't you Derrick?"

"Yes sir, I do."

"Yeah. It's all musty and wet smelling. The Peppers' cellar was like that. It was deep, too. Deeper than the storm cellar my parents have in their backyard. The wooden stairs creaked at first when we started down them. Then they just collapsed. The whole rickety staircase just fell. David was hurt pretty bad. One leg was broken and twisted around behind him. He had a broken arm, too. He was unconscious for a while.

"I had some bruises and a few cuts, but I was mostly okay. Scared shitless, but okay otherwise. I didn't know how the fuck we were going to get out of there. I could tell David was hurt pretty bad because of the way he was laying there with his leg behind him and the broken stairs all around him. But he was breathing and I couldn't do anything for him, so I started looking around.

"There were a whole bunch of jars down there. Mrs. Pepper canned stuff from their old garden, I guess. There were a lot of pickles and tomatoes. A lot. But there were some other jars, too."

Tim stopped talking. He stared at the ceiling in silence. Derrick saw that the patient's eyes were moist. A single tear spilled from one eye and ran down the side of his face and into his mussed brown hair.

"What was in them other jars, Mr. Baker?" he asked.

"Ears, Derrick. Ears. What did you think was in there?"

"I didn't know."

"See, so much of the truth has been forgotten," Tim said. "How long have I been in here?"

"Twenty-two years. Almost twenty-three is what I hear," Derrick said.

"Umm-hmm. Details are forgotten over time.

"Those jars were filled with ears. Big ears, little ears; adult ears and baby ears. Human fucking ears, Derrick. You hear what I'm saying?"

"I understand."

"It creeped me out to see those ears. They were canned like the pickles. They were packed in the glass jars but were able to float around a little bit in the...the juice or canning fluid or whatever it was. I don't know. I stared at those jars for a long time. Until David woke up and started screaming.

"I still couldn't do anything for him, no matter how much he screamed. I know he had to be hurting. I screamed, too. I screamed for help. But nobody could hear us. The neighbors weren't home. It was mid-afternoon and everybody who lived around there was at work. David asked me to move his leg. He didn't want his back laying on it. I did that. It must have hurt real bad because he passed out again.

"Then the sun started going down. It got real dark real fast in that cellar. When it was mostly dark, that's when I saw Warren Pepper sitting in the corner furthest from the door. God, I remember how the hair stood up on the back of my neck when I saw him sitting down there with his knees pulled up under his chin and half his head missing. He was wearing his army uniform. But half his fucking head was gone...his jaw was like a bowl holding this mush...mush that looked like that oatmeal you were feeding me except that it had red streaks in it.

"He moved. It was like he had been sitting there for a long, long time and had to get up real slow. But he got up. He stood up and took a step toward me. I remember pissing. I'd had to go for a while anyway. I just did it.

119

Pissed all over myself. I was so scared. Do you know what I mean?"

"I understand," Derrick said. "But, don't you think you was just imagining it? I mean, you was just a boy and you was scared anyway..."

"You're sounding like one of those prick doctors, Derrick. Don't do that. Just don't. He was real enough. Warren Pepper was there with me in his root cellar. You can bet your ass on that.

"He leaned over me and then he had his head back. It wasn't right. It was like somebody had tried to put the pieces of it back together. But they didn't fit together any more.

"'Hello, Timmy,' he said. Oh, he remembered me even though I'd just been a little kid when he was alive. 'I'm glad you dropped in,' he said. He laughed at that. 'I saw you looking at my ears. Do you know why I have those?' I guess I shook my head.

"'In 'Nam, we cut off the ears of those commie fucks,' Warren said. 'Some guys cut them off as trophies. Not me. I found a better use for them. I ate them, Timmy. You see, if you eat their ears you can hear the little gooks when they're sneaking up on you to shoot you in the back. I killed a lot of gooks while I was in 'Nam, Timmy. Lots of gooks. Old men, women, babies -- it didn't matter. They were all commie gooks that wanted to kill Americans. The more I killed, the more ears I collected. I couldn't possibly eat them all. I had to do it in secret. The other guys, they didn't believe in the power I got from eating the ears and they didn't want to know I was doing it.

"'My mom had taught me how to can vegetables when I was a boy. So I started canning me some ears, Timmy.

For later. There were dry spells when there just weren't any gooks to kill. That made me real nervous. It made me think I was losing my special power. So I kept a jar of gook ears in my pack all the time so I could eat them when there weren't any fresh ones...just so I'd know I wasn't losing the power to hear them coming up behind me or climbing a tree ahead of me. The snipers were the worst, Timmy. I lost a lot of buddies to snipers.'"

Tim Baker's eyes drifted from Derrick's patient face to the ceiling of the little room. His face took on a pinched, painful look -- his eyebrows knitted over his nose and his lips pressed tight.

"It's funny how I remember every word, isn't it?" Tim asked, turning his head to face Derrick again. "It's like Warren Pepper has become one of the voices I hear. But of course that isn't true. I can't hear him. At least, not over all the other screaming.

"'Do you want that power, Timmy?' He asked me that. 'Do you want to be able to hear them sneaking up on you so you can kill them before they kill you?' I told him nobody was sneaking up on me. 'That's where you're wrong, Timmy. See those ears?' He pointed to the jars. There were five jars of ears; I remember that now. He pointed to them and said, 'I killed the gooks attached to those ears, Timmy. They're in Hell now where their pinko commie souls belong. But they're still coming after you, Timmy. At night they come out of Hell looking for Americans. That's what they were bred for, what they lived their fucking lives for.'

"Then he took a jar off the shelf and opened it. He fished around in it and pulled out a little ear. It must have been a baby's ear. He held it out to me. I remember the smell, kind of like vinegar but with something rotten in it, like a dead mouse or something. I backed away but bumped into the wall. He came at me. Not fast, just slow, with that ear held out in front of him, level with my face.

"I screamed. Oh man, I screamed and screamed...until he shoved that ear into my mouth. I gagged and tried to spit it out, but he covered my mouth with his hand. He covered my nose and mouth with his hand and said he'd smother me if I didn't eat the damn ear. Do you hear me, Derrick? Do you hear how it happened?"

"I hear you, Mr. Baker. God help you."

"God? Leave Him out of this shit. I ate the fucking ear. I ate it. It was like chewing the most gristly piece of steak I'd ever had, except that it tasted like vinegar, too.

"But he was right. I could hear things I'd never heard before. But it was all a trick, you see. A nasty trick. I could just hear a little bit. Just enough to know there was more -- more that I couldn't hear yet. He gave me the jar and told me to keep eating and I'd be able to hear more. I'd be able to hear everything I wanted.

"I was scared. I was even more scared now that I could hear them a little. And I'd already eaten one. I ate another. And another. But the sounds I heard got worse. It was all screaming. I told him that all I could hear was people screaming like they were in pain. He laughed at me.

"'That's right, Timmy. You're hearing those commie gook mother fuckers burning in Hell. I did that. I put them there. You like it? I killed them all and sent them to Hell where they belong. Eat up and you'll hear more. Their screams are my victory song, Timmy. You need to hear the full choir.'

"I tried to run. I went to where the stairs had been, but of course I couldn't get out. I screamed for help again. David woke up. Warren Pepper was standing behind me, but I guess David couldn't see him. David just moaned and asked me to please help him. He said he thought he was going to die from the pain. That's when Warren Pepper whispered in my ear."

"'He's not in Hell,' he said, pointing to David. 'Eat his ear while he's still alive and it'll drown out the symphony of the damned. I know it gets to you after a while. It did me. That's why I ate my mom and dad's ears.'

"I looked at him then and saw that the top of his head was gone again. His hand reached out to me and there was a knife in it. A long butcher knife. Probably the same knife I'd seen him holding the day he killed himself. The knife he'd used to take his parents' ears. He put it in my hand and pointed to David again.

"Oh dear God. They were screaming in my head and I wanted them to stop. No matter how much I screamed I couldn't block them out. I just wanted them to stop. David was already hurt. I could say he cut his ear off in the fall." Tim paused. He sighed, but the sigh ended as a deep sob that caused his chest to strain against the canvas strap crossing his upper torso.

"I did it, Derrick. I cut off my best friend's ear and I ate it. It was warm and ... different than the canned ears ... not so rubbery. It tasted salty from the blood. David tried to fight me off, but he couldn't do much with just one good arm and leg. He passed out again before I'd finished sawing the ear off. The knife was dull.

"The screaming didn't stop. Not even when I cut off David's other ear and ate that, too. Warren Pepper just laughed at me when I did that.

"I could see stars in the sky when somebody finally found us. It was old man Miller, who lived next door to the Pepper house. Then my mom and dad were there looking down at us with David's mom. They said the fire department was coming to get us out. My mom was crying. So was David's mom. I don't think she could see anything but his legs from up there. She couldn't see his bloody head.

"A fireman came down to get us. I clung to him while he carried me up a ladder. The fresh night outside the cellar smelled so good. But still, I heard those dead Vietnamese people screaming in my head. I could hear David, too. He had died down there. The fireman was trying to put me down. My dad was trying to help peel me off the fireman. I saw the man's ear and just reacted. I wasn't myself any more. I ripped his ear off with my teeth and swallowed it whole.

"It didn't help. Nothing helps. They -- the police -- claim I ate all the ears in all five of those jars. That's a lie, Derrick. Warren Pepper ate most of those. He went after them like most people eat potato chips. Of course, nobody else ever saw Warren Pepper in the cellar that day. They tried to tell me that when they were determining whether or not I could stand trial for killing David and attacking the fireman. The police ... or lawyers ... or somebody was saying I'd planned the thing the whole time just to attack David. They said I knew about the ears and had been eating them for a long time. That's a load of shit. He was my best friend. I wouldn't have hurt him if it hadn't been for Warren Pepper. You believe me, don't you?"

Derrick didn't answer for a moment. Then he smiled slowly and nodded. "Yes sir, Mr. Baker. I believe you. I think you're a decent man."

"I never wanted--" Tim stopped when the door of his room opened and one of the pretty young nurses came in.

"Derrick, what are you still doing here?" she asked.

"I was just having a talk with Mr. Baker here," the big orderly answered. He looked back to the patient strapped in the bed. "It looks like it's time for some medicine for you and time for me to get home."

Tim cast a look over Derrick's shoulder toward the waiting nurse. Then he motioned with his head for the orderly to lean close.

"I never wanted to hurt anyone, Derrick. But the voices...the screams..."

The nurse ran from the room shrieking. It took two other nurses and another burly orderly to pull Tim Baker's mouth off Derrick's head. When they got the two men separated, Derrick's ear was gone. Where it had been there was only a dark hole leaking thick red blood.

Tim swallowed and turned his head away.

"I still hear them," he moaned. "They're still screaming."

A Drink from the Springs

Ben Redding leaned forward in his saddle and spat over the bank of Black Bear Creek. The dusty spittle was the only moisture covering the sun-cracked bed of the small, winding waterway. He lifted his stained hat and swiped a sleeve across his sweaty brow as a gust of dry, dirty wind swept through the tall prairie grass.

"Reckon Bogey Creek an Skel'ton Creek'll be bone dry, too," Franky, the younger of the two cowhands, said.

"Likely," Ben answered. He looked toward the sun. "'Bout four hours of good light left. You better head on back and tell the boss the creeks are dry. I'm going on ahead to see if the Salt Fork River has any water."

"That's a good forty miles," Franky announced.

"Yep. The herd'll probably still be close to the Cimarron. You can get there in time for supper."

"The Cimarron," Franky snorted. "Nothin' but a damn mudhole."

"Tell Will I'll be back late tomorrow. He might want to move the herd a little to the west, try to hit the lake in the salt plains. We'll lose a lot of beef if we have to do that." There was a moment of silence as the two men looked at the dry creek bed one more time. "Better go now," Ben said, then urged his horse down the bank and across the bottom of Black Bear Creek. He heard Franky turn around and start back the way they had come.

"Kid talks too much," Ben told his mare as they climbed the opposite bank. He pushed her into a trot and began covering ground on the parched earth of the Indian Nation, heading north.

He found Skeleton Creek just as the sun was leaving the sky. Except for a very few stagnant, shallow puddles, the creek was dry. Ben made camp for the night, keeping his rifle tucked up close to his body in case the redskins came to investigate him. He knew it wasn't likely; this was Cherokee country, but there had been bands of marauding Comanches reported back at the fort.

At daybreak he was back in the saddle and moving steadily across the changeless countryside. His throat begged for the last drops stored in his canteen, but he ignored it. His bowels, however, couldn't be put off any longer. At the closest growth of brush, he slid off the mare's back and hurriedly dropped his trousers.

When he emerged from the bushes, he was momentarily stunned to find he was alone. He looked around frantically, and soon saw the backend of his horse jogging away toward the north. Ben shouted at her, cursed her, and finally pleaded, but the mare never glanced back at him.

He started walking, going just fast enough to keep the horse in sight. He didn't dare go faster; it was far too hot to run. His canteen was strapped to his saddle, as was his rifle and most of his food. The mare never wavered, but kept moving at a steady, almost leisurely pace, as if she knew where she was going.

The sun reached its zenith and hovered, staring down at the stumbling, cussing man on the prairie. A stray cloud floated into the blazing blue of the sky, but the angry sun burned it to vapor before its shadow could touch the man.

Ben fell to his knees, staggered back to his feet and pushed himself forward. The mare's ass seemed to shimmer ahead of him as the heat rose in waves from the ground. Then she disappeared into a valley and Ben was forced to look at nothing but the motionless grass that waited for his dusty boots to trample it down on his way to a thirsty death.

After an eternity, he reached the crest of the valley and looked down into it.

Water!

A small lake lay winking up at him, the surface silvery in the bright afternoon sun. Trees, evergreens and maple mostly, stood sentinel around the edges of the water. The prairie sloped gently down toward the shore, and Ben tried to walk, but soon found himself rolling and sliding through the brittle grass toward the blessed water that awaited him. At the floor of the valley he regained his footing and ran as fast as he could make himself go.

Then he stopped dead, his feet suddenly as heavy as if they had taken root in the soil. Ben saw his mare laying on her side next to the water's edge. His nostrils filled with the coppery smell of fresh blood. A strange woman was standing in the water. Ben's eyes widened in disbelief as the woman bent forward and buried her face in the wound on his horse's throat. A sickening, sucking sound carried across to him and Ben felt his stomach roll over.

The woman looked up and her colorless eyes locked with those of Ben Redding. They studied one another; Ben confused over the long white hair and pale flesh of the beautiful, morbid woman. Her skin and hair were smeared with bright blood, which only served to highlight her severe whiteness all the more. Her shoulders were bare, and Ben wondered about the rest of her, but could not pull his gaze from the colorless depths of her eyes.

"I haven't eaten in weeks," the woman said. Her voice was like water lapping stones on a lake shore.

"My horse … " Ben said in a faltering voice.

The strange albino woman looked at him for a moment, as if she didn't understand, then smiled and reached into the mare's neck. She tore off a piece of flesh and extended the dripping offering to Ben.

"No," he said, turning away, sure he was going to cover the grass with his breakfast. "That ain't what I meant. I was gonna ride her, not eat her."

"Are you thirsty?" the woman asked. Ben's burning throat forced him to look back at her. He nodded. "Then come and drink," she waved a bloody hand over the surface of the water.

"Why is there water here?" Ben asked as he edged closer. "Creeks are all dry. Rivers are mostly dry."

"This lake is spring-fed," the woman answered in her weird, soft voice. "There are five springs here that bubble up from the dark places in the center of the world."

"How'd you kill her?" Ben asked, seeing no weapon the woman could have used to open the horse's throat.

"It wasn't hard," the woman laughed. "I was hungry."

"Aren't there any fish in there?"

"No, no fish."

"It's not poison, is it?"

She laughed again, but gave no answer.

"Maybe you'll swim with me?" she asked. She raised herself in the water, revealing her ample, snowy breasts. Ben stared in fascination at the round, pale nipples, and couldn't help but let his eyes travel down her belly to where the water licked at her navel. He loved a woman with good legs and tried to take advantage of the crystal-clear water to catch a glimpse of what waited below her waist, but curiously, he saw nothing at all.

"Come closer, come into the water," she said in a seductive whisper.

Ben's eyes slid from her beckoning, bloody hand to the corpse of his horse. He broke from his position so suddenly he startled himself. He snatched the canteen from his saddle and ran for a stand of thicker trees, his free hand gripping the butt of the revolver at his hip. He heard the woman's eerie laugh ring out behind him as he entered the shade of maples.

He tried to slow himself. Ben Redding was a man accustomed to the dry plains. He knew how to ration a small portion of water to last himself for days and days. But the canteen was soon empty and he found himself running his tongue around the inside of the opening to catch the last hint of moisture. Finally he dropped the container and peered out of the trees.

The woman was gone. Only the leaking body of his horse remained by the shore of the lake.

Ben waited in the trees until nightfall, arguing with himself about the grounds for his irrational fear. His mind knew that the woman in the lake had just been a little "touched" as the Indians said. But his heart insisted she was something more, and that she was waiting for him, eager to taste him the way she had tasted his horse.

When the sun had fallen from the sky and only the stars and a sliver of moon shone down on him, Ben moved quietly from the cover of the trees and edged toward the water. He dipped his canteen into the cool lake and heard it gurgle as it filled. His eyes roved the woods and grass around the shore, one hand always near his pistol. When the canteen was full, he pulled it from the water and reached down to screw on the cap.

His muscles suddenly loosened. He felt dizzy and swayed on his heels. He knew he was going to fall forward, and it was the thought, the horror of falling into the polluted water that anchored his brain and allowed him to regain control of his body.

The bottom of the lake was carpeted with bloated bodies. Whites, Indians, a few Negroes. Mostly men, but also women and children lay entombed below the glassy surface.

Eyes round with terror and a strange, choking sound coming from his gaping mouth, Ben turned quickly and ran. His open canteen, still clutched in a taut hand, sloshed liquid over his fingers as he pounded across the floor of the valley.

By dawn, the lake and all its strangeness was far behind. He had convinced himself the woman was only a lost crazy, and the bodies only visions brought on by his fear, hunger, and intense thirst. In his hurry to leave, he had lost nearly half the precious water from his canteen.

He was once more the calm, level-headed cattleman, second in command under Will Bond. He had a duty to perform. The herd of cattle was somewhere behind him on the plains of the Indian Nation, and it was up to him to find the water needed to make Dodge City, Kansas.

Soon the sun made it too hot to move, so Ben lay down in the shade of some brush to rest for a few hours before getting his bearings and trying to figure out how to get back to the herd.

He unslung the canteen from his shoulder and unscrewed the cap, forcing all images of the lake, the woman, and the bloated bodies from his mind. He lifted the container, tipping the opening toward his mouth, eager for the clear, cold water to splash the back of his throat.

"Yeessss … "

Ben froze. His eyes fixed on the small opening of the canteen. He could see the water rolling and sloshing within. His hand was steady; the canteen was not moving, and yet the water inside was active, as if eager to come out.

Slowly, Ben opened his hand and let the canteen fall to the ground. It made a solid thunk as it hit, then fell over. Water came rushing out to cover the hard earth of the prairie.

Ben stepped back, his mouth shaping inarticulate words as he watched every drop of water pull itself out of the canteen and onto the ground. Then the puddle shaped itself and stood to face him. He gaped at the two-foot-tall miniature of the albino woman from the lake. She extended her arms to him and smiled.

"Drink me," her tiny voice whispered. She advanced a step. Ben staggered back a step. The woman advanced two steps, then a third, moving faster. She came to within a few inches of Ben's dusty boots and prepared to pounce on him.

"No!" Ben's revolver jumped from the worn leather holster and spat burning lead at the small figure. The pale miniature woman jerked when the first bullet hit her, but the missile simply passed through her body with nothing more than a splash and a small gout of steam. The bullets came so rapidly, however, that the form finally broke apart and fell to the ground where it spread out in a glittering puddle.

Ben continued to stand, watching, his empty six-gun still pointed at the ground. When the water began to move and come together again, he broke and ran.

He ran until his legs ached and his sides were sending sharp jabs of pain throughout his body. Ben finally slowed, but only long enough to catch his breath and let the pain ease before resuming his former, frantic pace. He felt certain that somewhere behind him the small, white-haired figure of a woman was running through prairie grass taller than herself, trying to catch him.

Ben continued to run until the world swam in his vision, then he paused and jogged awhile. He heard a rustling noise behind him, and immediately broke into a run again. Within a few paces he stumbled and crashed to the ground. His eyes rolled up and he knew nothing for a long while.

When he awoke, it was to the sound of cattle lowing and shuffling somewhere close by. Ben heard a horse snort and stamp less than ten feet from where he lay in the shade of a covered wagon. A shape bent over him, blocking out the noon sun, and Ben shrank away.

"You awake, Ben?" The voice belonging to the shape was one he recognized. A male voice. The cook.

"Zeb?" he croaked.

"That's right." The black-bearded cook grinned, then straightened. "Will! He's awake now." Zeb leaned back down and offered a dipper full of water.

Ben took the dipper in a trembling hand. "From the barrel?" he asked, his eyes flicking to the container fastened to the side of the wagon. Zeb nodded.

"It's gettin' mighty low. Men don't get no more'n a dipperful a day." Ben drank, the whole while listening for a voice in the water.

"Ben? You okay?" The tall, lean form of Will Bond stood before him. The trail boss hunkered down to a squatting position and studied Ben with his sun-faded blue eyes.

"I guess I've been better." Ben tried to grin.

Will only nodded. "Did you find any water? We need it bad."

Ben couldn't answer at first. Finally he turned his face away and said, "No, I didn't find any water."

"Ben, what is it?" Will always knew when he wasn't being straight with him.

"I found water." Ben looked at his boss. "But ... but we can't go there."

"Why not?"

"It ... it ... " Ben looked into the weathered face and knew he couldn't explain the woman. "It's poison, Will. It killed my horse."

The trail boss looked at him for a long while, then finally nodded. "Okay. I'm gonna have to ride out. I sent Franky looking for water again when we found you yesterday evening. If there's a poisoned pond out there, he won't know it's bad till he drinks it."

"I'm going with you." Ben forced himself to his feet. Both Zeb and Will protested, but Ben insisted. "If I hadn't been asleep, I could have warned him. And, I know where it is. I can tell you if it's the right place. You can't drink that water. You can't."

"You can't be going off in the sun again," Zeb argued. Ben ignored him and went to the horses. He picked one out and borrowed a saddle. He was ready to ride when Will was.

"He started back up the trail you left." Will said, spurring his mount out of camp. Ben followed.

The heat was incredible and soon Ben found himself licking his swollen tongue across cracked lips as he swayed in the saddle. Only his determination to keep anyone from finding and drinking from the spring-fed lake kept him going.

They found Franky near dusk. What was left of the young cowhand was lying face down in the sod. He was nothing but a broken skeleton, recognizable only by the torn clothes he wore. Both men bent over the heap, Will lifting a dusty, broken rib bone.

"Marrow's gone right out of the bones," he said in an awed voice. "I've never seen anything strip the flesh off a man like this, and then break the bones to get to the marrow." He dropped the bone back onto the skeleton, where it crumbled and turned to dust. He stood and glanced around, as if looking for the killer but not expecting to see anything. "Ain't that your canteen?"

Slowly, Ben turned and looked into the grass behind him. His canteen lay uncapped and empty, but not in the same position he had left it. He had a sickening image of the water-woman crawling back into the container and waiting until some poor fool found it and took a cool drink. Ben looked back to the skeleton.

Where is she now?

"Something's moving over there," Will said. He started forward, his pistol in hand. Ben followed, his own gun drawn, though he had doubts about its effectiveness against what they would find.

The two men moved cautiously toward the spot where the tall grass was rapidly parting as something moved away from them. They separated and advanced quickly on the thing, one on each side, until they were level with the shifting grass, then they closed on it.

Ben shrieked like a woman when he saw the long, narrow puddle stretching before him, cutting through the prairie grass like a fish through the ocean. The amount of water had increased greatly from what he had held in his canteen, and Ben could still see streaks of pale red as the puddle shifted and flowed forward with the fluid of Franky's body added to it.

Ben turned and ran, jumping back into the saddle and setting spur to the horse. He heard Will slapping the rump of his own gelding as he tried to catch up in the mad dash away from the mysterious puddle that was moving quickly to the northwest, back to the spring-fed lake where dark things bubble up from the center of the world.

Grandpa Frost

NOVEMBER 12, 1999
Running for three days now.

NOVEMBER 13, 1999
Still running.

NOVEMBER 14, 1999
Ace and Thunder died today. The sled is light, but I know the other dogs won't last much longer.

NOVEMBER 15, 1999
Tired. So tired, but must keep going. Jock died late yesterday.

NOVEMBER 16, 1999
Hector is the only dog left. I had to abandon the sled. A polar bear ran past us today. I could count his ribs as he ran, but he never gave us a second glance. So cold. Must keep running, I'm sure Grandpa Frost is catching up.

The beard I had such a tough time growing is frozen so hard I can barely open my mouth to eat the tasteless, dried food I have left.

NOVEMBER 17, 1999

My toes have turned black with frostbite. Food is practically gone.

I'm afraid I'll never live to see my wife or son again. I can't warn them of what's coming. Linda, Monte, I'm sorry. I can't – Dear God, help them.

Must keep going.

NOVEMBER 18, 1999

I'm so cold. And hungry. I'm rationing the food, but even with just myself and Hector, we only have a couple days of eating left. That's allowing one meal a day. I'm wearing so much clothing I can barely move, but it's just not enough. Nothing will be enough.

At this point I have to assume I will never make it back to civilization. I feel like I have to leave some record of what happened; I may be the only one left of the crew that was there. I'm sure of it, really.

I can see the clouds of a blizzard that seems to be running ahead of Grandpa Frost. They're massed up behind me like the Dallas Cowboys' defensive line. Oh yeah, they're ready for the blitz. I'm camped beside a lake, or maybe it's the edge of a bay. I don't know, but it's already beginning to freeze around the edges as Grandpa Frost gets closer.

I hope this pitiful diary will be of use someday.

I wish I had the records that were lost. I didn't understand much of the stuff the scientists said or wrote, but I caught the gist of the matter. A dog trainer doesn't need to understand the geometry involved in the measurement of the Earth's axis or the angle of a meteorite's impact. If humanity survives this onslaught, the research would be helpful; it would provide some scientific proof to a mad tale. But I don't have it, so I have to record from memory. And speculation.

The beginning may really be in the Ice Age, but the beginning for me, for the modern world, was October 11, 1999.

I was in Alaska. I wanted to run a team in the next Iditarod race. Linda came with me, and of course, Monte, too. I've only been out of the Marines for five months; I was in charge of a K-9 Corps in Texas. I love dogs, especially working dogs, and having a sled team has been a dream of mine for years.

I was training my team when it all began. When I learned the United Nations was sending an international coalition of scientists to the North Pole to investigate the cause of the disasters, I volunteered and was accepted as the civilian commander of the K-9 division for the unit.

I'm glad I sent my family home to Texas. Maybe, just maybe, they'll have a chance to run farther south and possibly escape. I can only hope …

NOVEMBER 19, 1999

The clouds are closer and I'm even colder today than yesterday. I can't stay here long. Grandpa Frost is catching up, and I don't want to be sitting here, my story half done, when he catches me. Just a short rest, and then we'll run some more.

Back to the story.

October 11, 1999. Something like a month before that, I think it was, a major disturbance was recorded in the asteroid belt that is between Mars and Jupiter. Most of the scientists I worked with at the Pole actually witnessed the crash in the belt. Anyway, there was a major collision between some exceptionally large meteors, and the debris from that crash was sent flying through space. I was told this has happened before, but never with such a large amount of debris.

What is believed to be several hundred tons of meteorites crashed into the Arctic, very near the North Pole. Immediately, things changed on Earth.

I have to jump ahead here to tell some of what was learned in the short time our crew was on the site. What was suspected was proven to be true; the angle of the Earth's axis had shifted when the space debris crashed. I can scarcely imagine such an impact. Not even a string of cobalt bombs could produce such an effect.

Because of the shift in the Earth's axis, the balance between planet and moon was thrown off kilter, causing abnormal tides worldwide. Also, many icebergs drifted further south, where they melted and added their water to the oceans.

Melting. Oh, but that won't last. No. Grandpa Frost will re-freeze them soon enough.

Gotta move on now. Is Hector asleep or dead?

NOVEMBER 20, 1999

Hector is still with me. I feel sorry for him. I know he's suffering even more than me. His feet would be bleeding if I could chip the ice away from his worn-down pads.

What happened next? Oh, yeah, the earthquakes.

New fault lines were created from the impact of the space junk, and old lines were aggravated. Earthquakes rocked the globe, finally proving the pessimists right; California is now just a series of little islands off the Nevada coast. China gained a canyon that surpasses

America's Grand Canyon for size. Of course, they lost a few million citizens in the trade. Most of Vietnam is gone, and what is left is a salty swamp. A lot of the old coastal countries and states are like that now.

But then we have new land to make up for it. The Hawaiian Islands, for instance, are now a small continent. I heard on the international news before leaving for the Pole that there was talk of Atlantis returning to the surface. They'll never find it. They won't have time.

The meteorites that found their way to Earth had burned into the ice, which then re-froze. That sounds familiar to sci-fi fans, I know, but this is worse. The ice was very thick. Most of the meteorites were about twenty-five feet below the surface, and still glowing pretty good when we got there. The scientists, led by an Englishman named Penobst, thought they were sinking deeper.

A hasty village was built near the place where the largest pieces of the debris were sunk, a cluster of huts around a gasoline-powered generator.

I have to sleep. Just a couple of hours. Not too long. No, that wouldn't be good.

NOVEMBER 21, 1999

When I woke up today, the snow was falling. Just flurries. I outran them, but they'll catch me again. Is Monte warm and snug in his crib? Does Linda have the fireplace roaring? Do they have any idea what's happening?

Digging began as soon as our camp at the Pole was set. We were trying to get to the meteorites before they sank any further.

Nobody paid much attention to the ice around the meteorites. At first it wasn't considered odd, especially in

141

the excitement and confusion. The ice in about a ten-foot diameter around the meteorites was normal, but beyond that it was blue.

Dark, deep blue. Like a baby's eyes. And the blue moved, inch by inch, toward the meteorites.

By the time we had dug down five feet, the blue matter had closed around the glowing meteorites. The light caused by the space junk's heat was still visible, but muffled, like we were seeing it through a fog.

Oh, yeah, though I was the dog trainer, I was still called upon to do manual labor, such as digging. That's why I was there to see what was happening.

Everyone noticed the blue stuff closing around the rocks, but nobody thought it important enough to bother with; just an effect of the fast melting and re-freezing of the ice.

We continued digging. Penobst said he thought the meteorites had stopped sinking.

The glow of the meteorites faded and died. It wasn't a slow process. One minute they were still glowing red, then they flickered and became nothing but cold, dead rock.

And the blue in the ice was rising to the surface.

To be continued …

NOVEMBER 22, 1999

No out-running the snow now. It's still falling pretty light, but I know it'll pick up soon. I wouldn't mind so much if the food wasn't gone. Hector's given up sniffing my empty pockets.

Penobst was a very curious man. It was right and proper he died first. He stood in our hole in the ice, watching the blue matter rise to the top like a whale needing air. By the time he realized the ice was softening, his feet had broken through.

He should have gone completely under, but he didn't. Only his feet went, and them not even to the top of his boots.

Then, the ice re-froze.

Two of us, me and a French scientist, tried to pull him out, but he was stuck tight in solid ice.

Then, the ice opened under the Frenchman – I think his name was Limly. He became stuck, too, his screams mingling with Penobst's. I'm afraid that the screams of those two men will ring in my numb ears forever.

I jumped back before I was trapped, too. I was still holding the gloved hand of Penobst, and when I jumped back I felt his fingers break inside his gloves. They shouldn't have broken, but when they did, it was more like icicles snapping apart than the bones of fingers.

I didn't have time to think about Penobst's fingers. The blue under the ice was moving. It was coming toward us. We panicked and ran like rabbits.

Rabbits are delicious to eat. Oh, what I wouldn't give for a hot, spitted brace of hare right now. Oh God, I'm rambling and I still have so much to write.

NOVEMBER 23, 1999

No time for chit-chat. And definitely no time for stupid rambling. The snow is falling as fast as the temperature and my fingers hurt when I try to curl them around my pen. I have one match left. Maybe tomorrow I'll use it.

We gathered in one of the buildings. Those who had not seen what happened were quickly filled in.

Suggestions as to what the blue thing was began to be thrown around. At first, it was thought it may be a form of alien life that had crashed with the meteorites, but that idea was dropped when someone reminded us how the blue had closed around the hot debris. It was coming to them, not away from them. Somebody else mentioned how the blue mass had seemed to suck the heat from the space rocks, and I related how Penobst's fingers had broken.

An American named Mitchell thought maybe it was a remnant of some one-celled animal that evolved in the primordial seas at the dawn of creation and were then frozen as the Earth's crust solidified and the first Ice Age came, about 570,000,000 years ago. Then, when the ice retreated, these creatures, who had adapted to such extremes, retreated to the polar caps with the ice. He said they went with the ice because they had learned to move through it by melting it ahead of them. Mitchell went on to say that these creatures lived by drawing the body heat from fish they caught under the ice. I don't know. A month ago I would have roared with laughter over his idea. Now, I'm just not sure. Mitchell claimed to have evidence to support his theory in a Virginia lab, evidence he found while core drilling in Greenland.

Then our Russian cook, whose name was Borg, spoke. He told a tale I don't have time to recap in much detail, but I'll try to convey the heart of his story tomorrow.

NOVEMBER 24, 1999

Too tired to write much.

Borg said there were legends dating back to the times of Odin and Thor, of something living in the ice of Siberia. Something that lived on warmth. He said that there were tales of camp-fires being sucked into the snow and ice, as well as the people who sat around them. When he started talking about frost giants, he was silenced with harsh words.

His tale was, of course, dismissed as folklore.

I guess the more they talked, the less the men of science believed what they had seen, and then there were those who hadn't seen. By now, nearly all of them had become unbelievers. They decided they wanted to go back out and look at the bodies of Penobst and Limly. Most of the rest of us went, too.

Grandpa Frost had retreated and seemed to be gathered around the spot where the meteorites and the two men were frozen in the Earth.

Penobst and Limly were still standing. Both were dead, their blue faces frozen in ghastly screams. I looked from their faces to the mass under the ice. I thought of a cat, crouching, ready to spring.

The scientists, the fools, walked boldly over the ice, only one or two looking down nervously. I, and a few of the others, stayed back, just watching. Someone tried to pull Limly from his place in the ice. A sound like breaking sticks filled the air and Limly fell forward, his back and lower legs broken.

Tune in tomorrow for the bone-chilling conclusion, folks.

NOVEMBER 25, 1999

This is it. Tonight is to be my last night. The snow is so heavy I can no longer see two feet in front of me. I've found shelter, of sorts, in a tiny ravine – a Texas pothole.

I've used my last match to build a small fire. That should give Grandpa Frost incentive to hurry this thing up.

Hector knows this is the end.

The thing under the ice attacked before the sound of Limly's breaking bones had died on the frigid air.

The men of science saw it coming, but in their hurry, one of them slipped. They fell like dominoes. Some were trapped completely under the ice, and frozen as they struggled. Others were caught as they tried to rise, half in and half out of the ice. None of them escaped.

The rest of us broke and ran toward the two helicopters that stood just outside the ring of huts. My feet got tangled up with someone else's and we both came down. Only us two saw what happened with any perspective.

The screams of the trapped scientists were fading, and as the men became blue and brittle in their parkas, the mass under the ice grew.

Then it stretched. I thought of a cat again, a cat just waking from a long nap.

The thing reached the helicopters as they prepared to take off. It melted and re-froze the ice. One of the choppers was sunk to where only the whirling propeller was visible, the other just so the doors were sufficiently blocked. Inside, people pressed against the glass like trapped flies.

I was already moving. I ran to the kennels and hitched my dog team. We took off at a run, with only the emergency supplies that were kept on the sled at all times. No one tried to stop us; not many were left by that time.

The blue mass gave chase at first, but the dogs were fresh and strong, and I suppose Grandpa Frost wanted to finish with those he already had trapped. Maybe he knew he would catch me later.

I ran. And now here I am, with only one dog left and both of us too exhausted to go any further.

What is the mass under the ice?

I've thought about that. I call it Grandpa Frost, but maybe Count Frost would be a better title.

I think both Mitchell and Borg were right in their theories. After all, most folklore evolved from what can be proven to be a base of scientific fact.

He's close now. The snow under my fire is starting to turn blue. Bring it on, Gramps. Get it over with. Hector is growing agitated, but he still won't leave me. He really is man's best friend.

We all know of Jack Frost, the little elf that paints the leaves bright colors in the fall and glazes frost on our windows.

But what is he really doing?

Stealing the warmth. The life.

What about the frost giants of Nordic myth?

I think both are mythological descendants of this thing under the ice, this thing Mitchell thinks has been living on Earth since the planet was formed.

I think it has tried to conquer the Earth before, in those times we call the Ice Ages. What stopped it? I don't know. I think maybe the young planet shifted as it became more solid, more mature, so to speak, and the sun's warmth turned it back.

And now, the Earth has shifted again.

He's all around us now. I'm not sure, but I think the ice I'm sitting on is softer than it was a few minutes ago.

My campfire isn't warming me anymore.

Hector has lain down to accept his fate.

I will too. I'll wrap this pitiful diary back in its oil skin and throw it away so Gramps won't swallow it with me, then I'll lie close to Hector so that we can share our warmth to the end. He's all the family I have now.

I wish I was home in Texas with Linda and Monte. I wish I knew they would be safe.

Good luck, world.

– Guy Olsen

ABOUT THE AUTHOR

Steven E. Wedel lives in central Oklahoma with his wife
and most of his kids ... the ones who haven't grown up
enough to leave the den yet, anyway. He began writing in
the mid-1980s and has kept at it despite numerous
disappointments and setbacks. Steve has a bachelor's
degree in journalism from the University of Central
Oklahoma and a master's degree in liberal studies from the
University of Oklahoma. He has worked as a machinist,
bookseller, stock clerk, journalist, and public relations
specialist, but is now a high school English teacher most of
the year.

Visit him online at www.stevenewedel.com